MW00477811

Avenging Angels:
Ghost Stories by Victorian Women Writers

edited with an introduction
by Melissa Edmundson

Victorian Secrets 2018

Published by

Victorian Secrets Limited
32 Hanover Terrace
Brighton BN2 9SN

www.victoriansecrets.co.uk

Avenging Angels: Ghost Stories by Victorian Women Writers
First published in 2018

Introduction and notes © 2018 by Melissa Edmundson
This edition © 2018 by Victorian Secrets
Composition and design by Catherine Pope

Frontcover image © iStockPhoto.com/sdominick

A catalogue record for this book is available from the British Library.

ISBN 978-1-906469-64-1

CONTENTS

INTRODUCTION

The ghost story has always been a social expression. During the holiday season in Britain and America, family and friends gathered together in their homes and shared supernatural tales. As the nineteenth century progressed, ghosts increasingly found their way into popular journals, magazines, and newspapers. These stories were usually published, read, and generally valued for their ability to entertain, but writers also found the supernatural a convenient way to indirectly relate more subversive or socially taboo topics to a wider reading public. Women, in particular, adapted the ghost story to bring greater attention to issues involving gender, class, sexuality, race, and economic concerns. Literary ghosts during the Victorian period were thus taken out of the remote European castles and dark dungeons of earlier Gothic works and literally brought home to readers as hauntings began to take place in middle-class houses in both urban and rural areas. These apparitions evoked fear because they were relatable and could appear seemingly anywhere. Women writers took full advantage of this rising popularity of the Victorian ghost and used supernatural fiction to their financial advantage as well, selling their creative work to support themselves and their families. In this way, the short story has been an empowering form for women writers since the early nineteenth century. In the ghost story, women found their professional and social voices.

In Amelia B. Edwards's "The Four-Fifteen Express," a character remarks, "women are so clever, you know, at putting themselves inside people's motives." Indeed, relationships are at the heart of these supernatural tales, and the women represented in this collection expand the parameters of the ghost story by creating apparitions that represent problems that first arise in the world of the living. This idea of "purposeful" specters that have something to say about our world is a strength of women's supernatural fiction and remains a dominant theme throughout these stories. The supernatural world holds a mirror up to the natural one and shows humanity at its best and worst. In these stories there are unbreakable bonds, such as the lovers in Elizabeth Stuart Phelps's "Since I Died," or the surrogate mother/daughter relationship that finally resolves the haunting in Mary E. Wilkins's "The

Lost Ghost." In both stories, we see love transcending physical death. On the other hand, these stories also highlight emotional trauma and suffering as the ghosts emerge because of murder, revenge, and betrayal. Often, and perhaps even more disturbingly, these betrayals take place within families. In Violet Hunt's "The Prayer," Alice Arne declares, "I think there are worse things than ghosts." This statement proves true within the context of Hunt's story, as the spiritual death of Edward Arne represents not only a soulless man but the death of love in marriage, a "natural," everyday problem that Hunt sets as a supernatural story. These tales are all the scarier when we realize that the true sources of fear within them are very much grounded in the real.

Even the idea of what constitutes the various forms of the supernatural becomes a topic of debate as these writers explore and expand the definition of a "ghost." Edith Nesbit's "From the Dead," Gertrude Atherton's "The Striding Place," and "The Prayer" present reanimated dead bodies. In these stories, the unrestful soul temporarily finds itself inhabiting a body. The spirit then haunts this body (or is sometimes not present at all) as the troubled ghostly energy is reflected in the physical and emotional trauma of the ghastly corporeal. In "The Prayer," Hunt reverses the traditional concept of a ghost as an otherworldly "spirit" that returns to haunt. Likewise, "The Striding Place" features a debate between the two main characters over what constitutes a spirit and what form that spiritual energy can take after it leaves the living body. By the end of the story, Gifford's offhanded comment, "I should rather enjoy experimenting with broken machinery," returns with horrific significance. In Mary Elizabeth Braddon's "The Shadow in the Corner," the ghost has no physical body but exists as a "troubled mind" that "had haunted the room ever since. It was not the ghost of the man's body that returned to the spot where he had suffered and perished, but the ghost of his mind—his very self."

Other ghosts, such as Katharine Greaves in Lettice Galbraith's "In the Séance Room" and Ida Helmont in "From the Dead" represent a more powerful form of femininity that intimidates the men who betrayed them. Once victims in the world of the living, these dead women return as revenants to stand unflinchingly before their victimizers and accuse. Having been helpless in life, they refuse to play the role of victim after death. At the same time, the ghosts of women complicate and call into question issues of gender. In both of the above stories, the spectral women are referred to as "it." Katharine Greaves is denied her humanity because of her role as a sexual object, a plaything that can easily be disposed of and (at least temporarily) silenced by a brutal death. Yet, she also transcends the beauty and fragility of the human (female) body and becomes something beyond gender, an instrument of revenge as she stands before her killer: "Nearer and nearer 'it' came. Now it was close to him. He could feel the deathly dampness of its breath; those awful eyes were looking into his. The distorted lips parted—formed a single word. Was it the voice of a guilty conscience, or did that word really ring through and through the room—'Murderer!'" Likewise, Ida Helmont embodies and projects her own suffering when the physical signs of death are melded with a look of undying love as her estranged husband recalls: "It came straight towards the bed, and stood at the bed-foot in its white grave-clothes, with the white bandage under its chin. There was a scent of lavender. Its eyes were wide open and looked at me with love unspeakable."

Several of the stories chosen for this collection show how women writers dealt with topics thought to be beyond the imagination of a Victorian "lady writer." Gruesome crimes are described in detail, along with the nefarious motives behind them. Financial greed is at the heart of "The Four-Fifteen Express," in which a man is bludgeoned to death. Rosa Mulholland's "The Ghost at the Rath" tells of a femme fatale who resorts to murder and kidnapping to keep her inheritance. Innocent children become victims of greed in both G. M. Robins's "The House Which Was Rent Free" and Wilkins's "The Lost Ghost." The descriptions of child abuse in both stories still have the power to unsettle modern readers. The fate of the working classes who are financially and socially vulnerable is explored in "The Shadow in the Corner." Maria's repeated placement in the corner as a lonely and frightened servant and her hopeless existence at Wildheath Grange—as someone "educated above her station"—is perhaps even scarier than the ghostly shadow of a wasted life that haunts her attic bedroom. Both ghost and woman represent lost hopes.

Women's ghost stories also explore sexual freedom and frequently expose contemporary taboos regarding same-sex desire. In "Since I Died," the unnamed narrator's need for a more intimate contact with her lover—rendered in the lines, "If I dared step near, or nearer; if it were Permitted that I should cross the current of your living breath; if it were Willed that I should feel the leap of human blood within your veins; if I should touch your hands, your cheeks, your lips; if I dropped an arm as lightly as a snow-flake round your shoulder"—works on both a supernatural and natural level. The words that remain unspoken at the end of the story are nonetheless felt and understood by both women, whose mutual love for one another remains very much alive, though they are now physically separated by death. "The Striding Place" likewise portrays an unspoken emotional connection between two men that can be fully realized only after death, as the narrator tells us, "Weigall had loved several women; but he would have flouted in these moments the thought that he had ever loved any woman as he loved Wyatt Gifford." One of the greatest defining characteristics of these stories is how they convey fundamental emotions such as love, grief, jealousy, and loss. Though they are very much of their time, they also transcend it. This timeless quality is perhaps why we, as readers, keep returning to the ghost story.

The women included in this collection come from a variety of backgrounds. One commonality, however, is that each made successful careers as professional writers while simultaneously leading independent lives that often challenged Victorian notions of what a woman should be. Amelia B. Edwards (1831-1892) wrote numerous novels and became a leading Egyptologist in her day. She founded the Egypt Exploration Society and wrote two influential books on Egypt: *Untrodden Peaks and Unfrequented Valleys* (1873) and *A Thousand Miles up the Nile* (1877). Elizabeth Stuart Phelps (1844-1911) wrote over fifty volumes of fiction, poetry, and essays. Throughout her life, she campaigned for women's rights and animal rights. Phelps advocated clothing reform for women, and in *What to Wear?* (1873), she urged women to burn their corsets. Mary Elizabeth Braddon (1835-1915) gained fame as a pioneering writer of sensation fiction. She became one of the bestselling novelists of the Victorian period after the publication of *Lady Audley's Secret* in 1862. Braddon also worked as editor of *Belgravia* magazine for a decade while supporting her husband and children through her writing. Rosa Mulholland (1841-1921) wrote novels and poetry in addition to short fiction, and her early work appeared in Charles Dickens's *Household Words*. Her essay, "Wanted an Irish Novelist," which appeared in the *Irish Monthly* in July 1891, urged Irish writers to include more Irish-themed subjects in their work. Mulholland aimed much of her fiction at young women, incorporating themes that promoted their social and financial independence. Edith Nesbit (1858-1924) wrote fiction for children, but she also wrote poetry, drama, and worked as an editor. She was a founding member of The Fabian Society and served as editor of the society's journal. Profits from the sale of her published work supported her own family, as well as children from her first husband's extramarital affairs. Little is known of the life of Lettice Galbraith. Throughout the 1890s Galbraith published her work in popular fiction magazines, and in addition to her supernatural fiction, she published another short story collection, *Pretty Miss Allington and Other Tales* (1893). Her short fiction frequently features unconventional women protagonists. Gertrude Minnie Robins (1861-1939) published several bestselling novels as "Mrs. Baillie Reynolds." She was a leading member of London's Women Writers' Club and the Society of Women Journalists. Robins supported women's suffrage and worked to promote the careers of professional women. Mary Eleanor Wilkins Freeman (1852-1930) wrote novels, short fiction, poetry, essays, and literature for children. She was a prominent New England regionalist, and much of her work centers on the lives of women, who are often alone or unmarried, and the working classes. Gertrude Atherton (1857-1948) wrote novels, short fiction, and essays. She was active in the early film industry in California and wrote the screenplay for *Don't Neglect Your Wife* (1921). Her early novels were considered scandalous, particularly *Patience Sparhawk and Her Times* (1897). Atherton remained a lifelong feminist. Violet Hunt (1866-1942) was a novelist and short story writer. Many of her novels feature rebellious, unconventional heroines who are important examples of the emergence of the New Woman in Victorian fiction at the turn of the twentieth century. Hunt established herself as a leading literary hostess in London and remained dedicated to many feminist causes throughout her life, including her active role in the Women Writers' Suffrage League.

Though this selection of authors is by no means meant to be comprehensive, it is my hope that the stories included in this collection give a sense of how women incorporated social themes in their supernatural fiction. Ideally, these stories will lead readers to seek out other supernatural work by these women, as well as to discover the many other women (of Victorian times and beyond) who excelled at the ghost story.

Melissa Edmundson

SUGGESTIONS FOR FURTHER READING

Nicola Bown, Carolyn Burdett, and Pamela Thurschwell (eds.), *The Victorian Supernatural* (Cambridge: Cambridge University Press, 2004).

Julia Briggs, *Night Visitors: The Rise and Fall of the English Ghost Story* (London: Faber, 1977).

Lynette Carpenter and Wendy K. Kolmar, "Introduction," in *Haunting the House of Fiction: Feminist Perspectives on Ghost Stories by American Women* (Knoxville, TN: University of Tennessee Press, 1991), pp. 1-25.

Vanessa D. Dickerson, *Victorian Ghosts in the Noontide: Women Writers and the Supernatural* (Columbia and London: University of Missouri Press, 1996).

Dara Downey, *American Women's Ghost Stories in the Gilded Age* (Basingstoke and New York: Palgrave Macmillan, 2014).

Melissa Edmundson, "Women Writers and Ghost Stories," in *The Routledge Handbook to the Ghost Story*, Luke Thurston and Scott Brewster (eds.), (New York and London: Routledge, 2017), pp. 69-77.

___, *Women's Ghost Literature in Nineteenth-Century Britain* (Cardiff: University of Wales Press, 2013).

Simon Hay, *A History of the Modern British Ghost Story* (Basingstoke and New York: Palgrave Macmillan, 2011).

Rosemary Jackson, "Introduction," in *What Did Miss Darrington See?: An Anthology of Feminist Supernatural Fiction*, Jessica Amanda Salmonson (ed.), (New York: The Feminist Press, 1989), pp. xv-xxxv.

Nickianne Moody, "Visible Margins: Women Writers and the English Ghost Story," in *Image and Power: Women in Fiction in the Twentieth Century*, Sarah Sceats and Gail Cunningham (eds.), (London and New York: Longman, 1996), pp. 77-90.

Dorothy Scarborough, "Introduction," in *Famous Modern Ghost Stories* (New York and London: G. P. Putnam's Sons, 1921).

___, *The Supernatural in Modern English Fiction* (New York and London: G. P. Putnam's Sons, 1917).

Andrew Smith, *The Ghost Story, 1840-1920: A Cultural History* (Manchester: Manchester University Press, 2010).

Luke Thurston, *Literary Ghosts from the Victorians to Modernism: The Haunting Interval* (New York and London: Routledge, 2012).

Diana Wallace and Andrew Smith (eds.), *Female Gothic: New Directions* (Basingstoke and New York: Palgrave Macmillan, 2009).

Jeffrey Andrew Weinstock, *Scare Tactics: Supernatural Fiction by American Women* (New York: Fordham University Press, 2008).

ACKNOWLEDGEMENTS

I am grateful to Catherine Pope for her early support of this project and for her editorial and design work throughout the publication process. Editing an anthology of women's ghost stories has long been a wish of mine, and she helped that wish to become a reality. My thanks go as well to Sarah Meaney for her careful reading of the entire manuscript and for her many helpful comments and suggestions. I would also like to thank Jeffrey Makala for his comments on the Introduction.

ABOUT THE EDITOR

Melissa Edmundson specializes in nineteenth and early twentieth-century British women writers, with a particular interest in women's ghost stories. She is the editor of a critical edition of Alice Perrin's *East of Suez* (1901), published by Victorian Secrets in 2011, and author of *Women's Ghost Literature in Nineteenth-Century Britain* (University of Wales Press, 2013) and *Women's Colonial Gothic Writing, 1850-1930: Haunted Empire* (Palgrave Macmillan, 2018). Her recent work includes essays on the First World War ghost stories of H. D. Everett and haunted objects in the supernatural fiction of Margery Lawrence, as well as a chapter on women writers and ghost stories for *The Routledge Handbook to the Ghost Story*.

Avenging Angels

Dedicated to the women writers who forged new paths and continue to show us what the ghost story can do.

THE FOUR-FIFTEEN EXPRESS*

Amelia B. Edwards

Chapter I

The events which I am about to relate took place between nine and ten years ago. Sebastopol had fallen in the early Spring; the peace of Paris had been concluded since March; our commercial relations with the Russian empire were but recently renewed; and I, returning home after my first northward journey since the war, was well pleased with the prospect of spending the month of December under the hospitable and thoroughly English roof of my excellent friend Jonathan Jelf, Esquire, of Dumbleton Manor, Clayborough, East Anglia. Travelling in the interests of the well-known firm in which it is my lot to be a junior partner, I had been called upon to visit not only the capitals of Russia and Poland, but had found it also necessary to pass some weeks among the trading ports of the Baltic; whence it came that the year was already far spent before I again set foot on English soil, and that instead of shooting pheasants with him, as I had hoped, in October, I came to be my friend's guest during the more genial Christmas-tide.

My voyage over, and a few days given up to business in Liverpool and London, I hastened down to Clayborough with all the delight of a schoolboy whose holidays are at hand. My way lay by the Great East Anglian line as far as Clayborough station, where I was to be met by one of the Dumbleton carriages and conveyed across the remaining nine miles of country. It was a foggy afternoon, singularly warm for the fourth of December, and I had arranged to leave London by the 4.15 Express. The early darkness of Winter had already closed in; the lamps were lighted in the carriages; a clinging damp dimmed the windows, adhered to the door-handles, and pervaded all the atmosphere; while the gas jets at the neighbouring bookstand

* "The Four-Fifteen Express" was published in *Routledge's Christmas Annual* in December 1866 and appears in Volume 3 of Edwards's collection *Monsieur Maurice and Other Tales* (London: Hurst and Blackett, 1873). The current text is based on the 1873 edition. Obvious typographical errors and inconsistencies have been silently corrected.

diffused a luminous haze that only served to make the gloom of the terminus more visible. Having arrived some seven minutes before the starting of the train, and, by the connivance of the guard, taken sole possession of an empty compartment, I lighted my travelling lamp, made myself particularly snug, and settled down to the undisturbed enjoyment of a book and a cigar. Great, therefore, was my disappointment when, at the last moment, a gentleman came hurrying along the platform, glanced into my carriage, opened the locked door with a private key, and stepped in.

It struck me at the first glance that I had seen him before—a tall, spare man, thin-lipped, light-eyed, with an ungraceful stoop in the shoulders, and scant grey hair worn somewhat long upon the collar. He carried a light waterproof coat, an umbrella, and a large brown japanned deed-box, which last he placed under the seat. This done, he felt carefully in his breast-pocket, as if to make certain of the safety of his purse or pocket-book; laid his umbrella in the netting overhead; spread the waterproof across his knees; and exchanged his hat for a travelling cap of some Scotch material. By this time the train was moving out of the station, and into the faint grey of the wintry twilight beyond.

I now recognised my companion. I recognised him from the moment when he removed his hat and uncovered the lofty, furrowed, and somewhat narrow brow beneath. I had met him, as I distinctly remembered, some three years before, at the very house for which, in all probability, he was now bound like myself. His name was Dwerrihouse; he was a lawyer by profession; and, if I was not greatly mistaken, was first cousin to the wife of my host. I knew also that he was a man eminently "well to do," both as regarded his professional and private means. The Jelfs entertained him with that sort of observant courtesy which falls to the lot of the rich relation; the children made much of him; and the old butler, albeit somewhat surly "to the general," treated him with deference. I thought, observing him by the vague mixture of lamplight and twilight, that Mrs. Jelf's cousin looked all the worse for the three years' wear and tear which had gone over his head since our last meeting. He was very pale, and had a restless light in his eye that I did not remember to have observed before. The anxious lines, too, about his mouth were deepened, and there was a cavernous hollow look about his cheeks and temples which seemed to speak of sickness or sorrow. He had glanced at me as he came in, but without any gleam of recognition in his face. Now he glanced again, as I fancied, somewhat doubtfully. When he did so for the third or fourth time, I ventured to address him.

"Mr. John Dwerrihouse, I think?"

"That is my name," he replied.

"I had the pleasure of meeting you at Dumbleton about three years ago."

Mr. Dwerrihouse bowed.

"I thought I knew your face," he said. "But your name, I regret to say—"

"Langford—William Langford. I have known Jonathan Jelf since we were boys together at Merchant Taylor's, and I generally spend a few weeks at Dumbleton in the shooting season. I suppose we are bound for the same destination?"

"Not if you are on your way to the Manor," he replied. "I am travelling upon business—rather troublesome business, too—whilst you, doubtless, have only pleasure in view."

"Just so. I am in the habit of looking forward to this visit as to the brightest three weeks in all the year."

"It is a pleasant house," said Mr. Dwerrihouse.

"The pleasantest I know."

"And Jelf is thoroughly hospitable."

"The best and kindest fellow in the world!"

"They have invited me to spend Christmas week with them," pursued Mr. Dwerrihouse, after a moment's pause.

"And you are coming?"

"I cannot tell. It must depend on the issue of this business which I have in hand. You have heard, perhaps, that we are about to construct a branch line from Blackwater to Stockbridge."

I explained that I had been for some months away from England, and had therefore heard nothing of the contemplated improvement.

Mr. Dwerrihouse smiled complacently.

"It *will* be an improvement," he said; "a great improvement. Stockbridge is a flourishing town, and needs but a more direct railway communication with the metropolis to become an important centre of commerce. This branch was my own idea. I brought the project before the board, and have myself superintended the execution of it up to the present time."

"You are an East Anglian director, I presume?"

"My interest in the company," replied Mr. Dwerrihouse, "is threefold. I am a director; I am a considerable shareholder; and, as head of the firm of Dwerrihouse,

Dwerrihouse, and Craik, I am the company's principal solicitor."

Loquacious, self-important, full of his pet project, and apparently unable to talk on any other subject, Mr. Dwerrihouse then went on to tell of the opposition he had encountered and the obstacles he had overcome in the cause of the Stockbridge branch. I was entertained with a multitude of local details and local grievances. The rapacity of one squire; the impracticability of another; the indignation of the rector whose glebe was threatened; the culpable indifference of the Stockbridge townspeople, who could *not* be brought to see that their most vital interests hinged upon a junction with the Great East Anglian line; the spite of the local newspaper; and the unheard-of difficulties attending the Common question, were each and all laid before me with a circumstantiality that possessed the deepest interest for my excellent fellow-traveller, but none whatever for myself. From these, to my despair, he went on to more intricate matters: to the approximate expenses of construction per mile; to the estimates sent in by different contractors; to the probable traffic returns of the new line; to the provisional clauses of the new Act as enumerated in Schedule D of the company's last half-yearly report; and so on, and on, and on till my head ached, and my attention flagged, and my eyes kept closing in spite of every effort that I made to keep them open. At length I was roused by these words:—

"Seventy-five thousand pounds, cash down."

"Seventy-five thousand pounds, cash down," I repeated, in the liveliest tone I could assume. "That is a heavy sum."

"A heavy sum to carry here," replied Mr. Dwerrihouse, pointing significantly to his breast-pocket; "but a mere fraction of what we shall ultimately have to pay."

"You do not mean to say that you have seventy-five thousand pounds at this moment upon your person?" I exclaimed.

"My good sir, have I not been telling you so for the last half hour?" said Mr. Dwerrihouse, testily. "That money has to be paid over at half-past eight o'clock this evening, at the office of Sir Thomas's solicitors, on completion of the deed of sale."

"But how will you get across by night from Blackwater to Stockbridge with seventy-five thousand pounds in your pocket?"

"To Stockbridge!" echoed the lawyer. "I find I have made myself very imperfectly understood. I thought I had explained how this sum only carries our new line only as far as Mallingford—the first stage, as it were, of our journey—and how our route from Blackwater to Mallingford lies entirely through Sir Thomas Liddell's property."

"I beg your pardon," I stammered. "I fear my thoughts were wandering. So you only go as far as Mallingford to-night?"

"Precisely. I shall get a conveyance from the 'Blackwater Arms.' And you?"

"Oh, Jelf sends a trap to meet me at Clayborough. Can I be the bearer of any message from you?"

"You may say if you please, Mr. Langford, that I wished I could have been your companion all the way, and that I will come over if possible before Christmas."

"Nothing more?"

Mr. Dwerrihouse smiled grimly.

"Well," he said, "you may tell my cousin that she need not burn the hall down in my honour *this* time, and that I shall be obliged if she will order the blue-room chimney to be swept before I arrive."

"That sounds tragic. Had you a conflagration on the occasion of your last visit to Dumbleton?"

"Something like it. There had been no fire lighted in my bedroom since the spring, the flue was foul, and the rooks had built in it; so when I went up to dress for dinner, I found the room full of smoke, and the chimney on fire. Are we already at Blackwater?"

The train had gradually come to a pause while Mr. Dwerrihouse was speaking, and on putting my head out of the window, I could see the station some few hundred yards ahead. There was another train before us blocking the way, and the ticket-taker was making use of the delay to collect the Blackwater tickets. I had scarcely ascertained our position, when the ruddy-faced official appeared at our carriage door.

"Ticket, sir!" said he.

"I am for Clayborough," I replied, holding out the tiny pink card.

He took it; glanced at it by the light of his little lantern; gave it back; looked, as I fancied, somewhat sharply at my fellow-traveller, and disappeared.

"He did not ask for yours," I said with some surprise.

"They never do," replied Mr. Dwerrihouse. "They all know me; and of course, I travel free."

"Blackwater! Blackwater!" cried the porter, running along the platform beside us, as we glided into the station.

Mr. Dwerrihouse pulled out his deed box, put his travelling-cap in his pocket, resumed his hat, took down his umbrella, and prepared to be gone.

"Many thanks, Mr. Langford, for your society," he said, with old-fashioned courtesy. "I wish you a good evening."

"Good evening," I replied, putting out my hand.

But he either did not see it, or did not choose to see it, and, slightly lifting his hat, stepped out upon the platform. Having done this, he moved slowly away, and mingled with the departing crowd.

Leaning forward to watch him out of sight, I trod upon something which proved to be a cigar-case. It had fallen, no doubt, from the pocket of his water-proof coat, and was made of dark morocco leather, with a silver monogram upon the side. I sprang out of the carriage just as the guard came up to lock me in.

"Is there one minute to spare?" I asked eagerly. "The gentleman who travelled down with me from town has dropped his cigar-case—he is not yet out of the station!"

"Just a minute and a half, sir," replied the guard. "You must be quick."

I dashed along the platform as fast as my feet could carry me. It was a large station, and Mr. Dwerrihouse had by this time got more than halfway to the farther end.

I, however, saw him distinctly, moving slowly with the stream. Then, as I drew nearer, I saw that he had met some friend—that they were talking as they walked—that they presently fell back somewhat from the crowd, and stood aside in earnest conversation. I made straight for the spot where they were waiting. There was a vivid gas-jet just above their heads, and the light fell full upon their faces. I saw both distinctly—the face of Mr. Dwerrihouse and the face of his companion. Running, breathless, eager as I was, getting in the way of porters and passengers, and fearful every instant lest I should see the train going on without me, I yet observed that the new-comer was considerably younger and shorter than the director, that he was sandy-haired, mustachioed, small-featured, and dressed in a close-cut suit of Scotch tweed. I was now within a few yards of them. I ran against a stout gentleman—I was nearly knocked down by a luggage-truck—I stumbled over a carpet-bag—I gained the spot just as the driver's whistle warned me to return.

To my utter stupefaction they were no longer there. I had seen them but two seconds before—and they were gone! I stood still. I looked to right and left. I saw no sign of them in any direction. It was as if the platform had gaped and swallowed them.

"There were two gentlemen standing here a moment ago," I said to a porter at my elbow; "which way can they have gone?"

"I saw no gentlemen, sir," replied the man.

The whistle shrilled out again. The guard, far up the platform, held up his arm, and shouted to me to "Come on!"

"If you're going on by this train, sir," said the porter, "you must run for it."

I did run for it—just gained the carriage as the train began to move—was shoved in by the guard, and left breathless and bewildered, with Mr. Dwerrihouse's cigar-case still in my hand.

It was the strangest disappearance in the world. It was like a transformation trick in a pantomime. They were there one moment—palpably there—talking—with the gaslight full upon their faces; and the next moment they were gone. There was no door near—no window—no staircase. It was a mere slip of barren platform, tapestried with big advertisements. Could anything be more mysterious?

It was not worth thinking about; and yet, for my life, I could not help pondering upon it—pondering, wondering, conjecturing, turning it over and over in my mind, and beating my brains for a solution of the enigma. I thought of it all the way from Blackwater to Clayborough. I thought of it all the way from Clayborough to Dumbleton, as I rattled along the smooth highway in a trim dog-cart drawn by a splendid black mare, and driven by the silentest and dapperest of East Anglian grooms.

We did the nine miles in something less than an hour, and pulled up before the lodge-gates just as the church clock was striking half-past seven. A couple of minutes more, and the warm glow of the lighted hall was flooding out upon the gravel; a hearty grasp was on my hand; and a clear jovial voice was bidding me "Welcome to Dumbleton."

"And now, my dear fellow," said my host, when the first greeting was over, "you have no time to spare. We dine at eight, and there are people coming to meet you; so you must just get the dressing business over as quickly as may be. By the way, you will meet some acquaintances. The Biddulphs are coming, and Prendergast (Prendergast, of the Skirmishers) is staying in the house. Adieu! Mrs. Jelf will be expecting you in the drawing-room."

I was ushered to my room—not the blue room, of which Mr. Dwerrihouse had made disagreeable experience, but a pretty little bachelor's chamber, hung with a delicate chintz, and made cheerful by a blazing fire. I unlocked my portmanteau. I tried to be expeditious; but the memory of my railway adventure haunted me. I could not get free of it. I could not shake it off. It impeded me—it worried me—it tripped me up—it caused me to mislay my studs—to mistie my cravat—to wrench the buttons off my gloves. Worst of all, it made me so late that the party had all assembled before I reached the drawing-room. I had scarcely paid my respects to Mrs. Jelf when dinner was announced, and we paired off, some eight or ten couples strong, into the dining-room.

I am not going to describe either the guests or the dinner. All provincial parties bear the strictest family resemblance, and I am not aware that an East Anglian banquet offers any exception to the rule. There was the usual country baronet and his wife; there were the usual country parsons and their wives; there was the sempiternal turkey and haunch of venison. *Vanitas vanitatum.* There is nothing new under the sun.

I was placed about midway down the table. I had taken one rector's wife down to dinner, and I had another at my left hand. They talked across me, and their talk was about babies. It was dreadfully dull. At length there came a pause. The entrées had just been removed, and the turkey had come upon the scene. The conversation had all along been of the languidest, but at this moment it happened to have stagnated altogether. Jelf was carving the turkey. Mrs. Jelf looked as if she was trying to think of something to say. Everybody else was silent. Moved by an unlucky impulse, I thought I would relate my adventure.

"By the way, Jelf," I began, "I came down part of the way today with a friend of yours."

"Indeed!" said the master of the feast, slicing scientifically into the breast of the turkey. "With whom, pray?"

"With one who bade me tell you that he should, if possible, pay you a visit before Christmas."

"I cannot think who that could be," said my friend, smiling.

"It must be Major Thorp," suggested Mrs. Jelf.

I shook my head.

"It was not Major Thorp," I replied. "It was a near relation of your own, Mrs. Jelf."

"Then I am more puzzled than ever," replied my hostess. "Pray tell me who it was."

"It was no less a person than your cousin, Mr. John Dwerrihouse."

Jonathan Jelf laid down his knife and fork. Mrs. Jelf looked at me in a strange, startled way, and said never a word.

"And he desired me to tell you, my dear madam, that you need not take the trouble to burn the Hall down in his honour this time; but only to have the chimney of the blue room swept before his arrival."

Before I had reached the end of my sentence, I became aware of something ominous in the faces of the guests. I felt I had said something which I had better have left unsaid, and that for some unexplained reason my words had evoked a general consternation. I sat confounded, not daring to utter another syllable, and for at least two whole minutes there was dead silence round the table.

Then Captain Prendergast came to the rescue.

"You have been abroad for some months, have you not, Mr. Langford?" he said, with the desperation of one who flings himself into the breach. "I heard you had been to Russia. Surely you have something to tell us of the state and temper of the country after the war?"

I was heartily grateful to the gallant Skirmisher for this diversion in my favour. I answered him, I fear, somewhat lamely; but he kept the conversation up, and presently one or two others joined in, and so the difficulty, whatever it might have been, was bridged over. Bridged over, but not repaired. A something, an awkwardness, a visible constraint remained. The guests hitherto had been simply dull; but now they were evidently uncomfortable and embarrassed.

The dessert had scarcely been placed upon the table when the ladies left the room. I seized the opportunity to drop into a vacant chair next Captain Prendergast.

"In Heaven's name," I whispered, "what was the matter just now? What had I said?"

"You mentioned the name of John Dwerrihouse."

"What of that? I had seen him not two hours before."

"It is a most astounding circumstance that you should have seen him," said Captain Prendergast. "Are you sure it was he?"

"As sure as of my own identity. We were talking all the way between London and Blackwater. But why does that surprise you?"

"*Because*," replied Captain Prendergast, dropping his voice to the lowest whisper—"*because John Dwerrihouse absconded three months ago, with seventy-five thousand pounds of the Company's money, and has never been heard of since.*"

Chapter II

John Dwerrihouse had absconded three months ago—and I had seen him only a few hours back. John Dwerrihouse had embezzled seventy-five thousand pounds of the company's money—yet told me that he carried that sum upon his person. Were ever facts so strangely incongruous, so difficult to reconcile? How should he have ventured again into the light of day? How dared he show himself along the line? Above all, what had he been doing throughout those mysterious three months of disappearance?

Perplexing questions these. Questions which at once suggested themselves to the minds of all concerned, but which admitted of no easy solution. I could find no reply to them. Captain Prendergast had not even a suggestion to offer. Jonathan Jelf, who seized the first opportunity of drawing me aside and learning all that I had to tell, was more amazed and bewildered than either of us. He came to my room that night when all the guests were gone, and we talked the thing over from every point of view—without, it must be confessed, arriving at any kind of conclusion.

"I do not ask you," he said, "whether you can have mistaken your man. That is impossible."

"As impossible as that I should mistake some stranger for yourself."

"It is not a question of looks or voice, but of facts. That he should have alluded to the fire in the blue room is proof enough of John Dwerrihouse's identity. How did he look?"

"Older, I thought. Considerably older, paler, and more anxious."

"He has had enough to make him look anxious, anyhow," said my friend, gloomily; "be he innocent or guilty."

"I am inclined to believe that he is innocent," I replied. "He showed no embarrassment when I addressed him, and no uneasiness when the guard came round. His conversation was open to a fault. I might almost say that he talked too freely of the business which he had in hand."

"That again is strange; for I know no one more reticent on such subjects. He actually told you that he had the seventy-five thousand pounds in his pocket?"

"He did."

"Humph! My wife has an idea about it, and she may be right—"

"What idea?"

"Well, she fancies—women are so clever, you know, at putting themselves inside people's motives—she fancies that he was tempted; that he did actually take the money; and that he has been concealing himself these three months in some wild part of the country—struggling possibly with his conscience all the time, and daring neither to abscond with his booty, nor to come back and restore it."

"But now that he has come back?"

"That is the point. She conceives that he has probably thrown himself upon the Company's mercy; made restitution of the money; and, being forgiven, is permitted to carry the business through as if nothing whatever had happened."

"The last," I replied, "is an impossible case. Mrs. Jelf thinks like a generous and delicate-minded woman, but not in the least like a board of railway directors. They would never carry forgiveness so far."

"I fear not; and yet it is the only conjecture that bears a semblance of likelihood. However, we can run over to Clayborough to-morrow, and see if anything is to be learned. By the way, Prendergast tells me you picked up his cigar-case."

"I did—and here it is."

Jelf took the cigar-case, examined it, and said at once that it was beyond doubt Mr. Dwerrihouse's property, and that he remembered to have seen him use it.

"Here, too, is his monogram on the side," he added. "A big J transfixing a capital D. He used to carry the same on his note paper."

"It proves, at all events, that I was not dreaming."

"Ay; but it is time you were asleep and dreaming now. I am ashamed to have kept you up so long. Good night."

"Good night, and remember that I am more than ready to go with you to Clayborough, or Blackwater, or London, or anywhere, if I can be of the least service."

"Thanks! I know you mean it, old friend, and it may be that I shall put you to the test. Once more, good night."

So we parted for that night, and met again in the breakfast-room at half-past eight next morning. It was a hurried, silent, uncomfortable meal. None of us had slept well, and all were thinking of the same subject. Mrs. Jelf had evidently been crying; Jelf was impatient to be off; and both Captain Prendergast and myself felt ourselves to be in the painful position of outsiders, who are involuntarily brought into a domestic trouble. Within twenty minutes after we had left the breakfast-table, the dog-cart was brought round, and my friend and I were on the road to Clayborough.

"Tell you what it is, Langford," he said, as we sped along between the wintry hedges, "I do not much fancy to bring up Dwerrihouse's name at Clayborough. All the officials know that he is my wife's relation, and the subject just now is hardly a pleasant one. If you don't much mind, we will take the 11.10 to Blackwater. It's an important station, and we shall stand a far better chance of picking up information there than at Clayborough."

So we took the 11.10, which happened to be an express, and, arriving at Blackwater about a quarter before twelve, proceeded at once to prosecute our inquiry.

We began by asking for the station-master—a big, blunt, business-like person, who at once averred that he knew Mr. John Dwerrihouse perfectly well, and that there was no director on the line whom he had seen and spoken to so frequently.

"He used to be down here two or three times a week, about three months ago," said he, "when the new line was first set afoot; but since then, you know, gentlemen—"

He paused, significantly.

Jelf flushed scarlet.

"Yes, yes," he said hurriedly, "we know all about that. The point now to be ascertained is whether anything has been seen or heard of him lately."

"Not to my knowledge," replied the station-master.

"He is not known to have been down the line any time yesterday, for instance?"

The station-master shook his head.

"The East Anglian, sir," said he, "is about the last place where he would dare to show himself. Why, there isn't a station-master, there isn't a guard, there isn't a porter, who doesn't know Mr. Dwerrihouse by sight as well as he knows his own face in the looking-glass; or who wouldn't telegraph for the police as soon as he had set eyes on him at any point along the line. Bless you, sir! There's been a standing order out against him ever since the twenty-fifth of September last."

"And yet," pursued my friend, "a gentleman who travelled down yesterday from London to Clayborough by the afternoon Express, testifies that he saw Mr. Dwerrihouse in the train, and that Mr. Dwerrihouse alighted at Blackwater station."

"Quite impossible, sir," replied the station-master, promptly.

"Why impossible?"

"Because there is no station along the line where he is so well known, or where he would run so great a risk. It would be just running his head into the lion's mouth. He would have been mad to come nigh Blackwater station; and if he had come, he would have been arrested before he left the platform."

"Can you tell me who took the Blackwater tickets of that train?"

"I can, sir. It was the guard—Benjamin Somers."

"And where can I find him?"

"You can find him, sir, by staying here, if you please, till one o'clock. He will be coming through with the up Express from Crampton, which stays at Blackwater for ten minutes."

We waited for the up Express, beguiling the time as best we could by strolling along the Blackwater road till we came almost to the outskirts of the town, from which the station was distant nearly a couple of miles. By one o'clock we were back again upon the platform, and waiting for the train. It came punctually, and I at once recognised the ruddy-faced guard who had gone down with my train the evening before.

"The gentlemen want to ask you something about Mr. Dwerrihouse, Somers," said the station-master, by way of introduction.

The guard flashed a keen glance from my face to Jelf's, and back again to mine.

"Mr. John Dwerrihouse, the late director?" said he, interrogatively.

"The same," replied my friend. "Should you know him if you saw him?"

"Anywhere, sir."

"Do you know if he was in the 4.15 Express yesterday afternoon?"

"He was not, sir."

"How can you answer so positively?"

"Because I looked into every carriage, and saw every face in that train, and I could take my oath that Mr. Dwerrihouse was not in it. This gentleman was," he added, turning sharply upon me. "I don't know that I ever saw him before in my life, but I remember *his* face perfectly. You nearly missed taking your seat in time at this station, sir, and you got out at Clayborough."

"Quite true," I replied; "but do you not also remember the face of the gentleman who travelled down in the same carriage with me as far as here?"

"It was my impression, sir, that you travelled down alone," said Somers, with a look of some surprise.

"By no means. I had a fellow-traveller as far as Blackwater, and it was in trying to restore him the cigar-case which he had dropped in the carriage, that I so nearly let you go on without me."

"I remember your saying something about a cigar-case, certainly," replied the guard, "but——"

"You asked for my ticket just before we entered the station."

"I did, sir."

"Then you must have seen him. He sat in the corner next the very door to which you came."

"No, indeed. I saw no one."

I looked at Jelf. I began to think the guard was in the ex-director's confidence, and paid for his silence.

"If I had seen another traveller I should have asked for his ticket," added Somers. "Did you see me ask for his ticket, sir?"

"I observed that you did not ask for it, but he explained that by saying——."

I hesitated. I feared I might be telling too much, and so broke off abruptly.

The guard and the station-master exchanged glances. The former looked impatiently at his watch.

"I am obliged to go on in four minutes more, sir," he said.

"One last question, then," interposed Jelf, with a sort of desperation. "If this gentleman's fellow-traveller had been Mr. John Dwerrihouse, and he had been sitting in the corner next the door by which you took the tickets, could you have failed to see and recognise him?"

"No, sir; it would have been quite impossible."

"And you are certain you did *not* see him?"

"As I said before, sir, I could take my oath I did not see him. And if it wasn't that I don't like to contradict a gentleman, I would say I could also take my oath that this gentleman was quite alone in the carriage the whole way from London to Clayborough. Why, sir," he added, dropping his voice so as to be inaudible to the station-master, who had been called away to speak to some person close by, "you expressly asked me to give you a compartment to yourself, and I did so. I locked you in, and you were so good as to give me something for myself."

"Yes; but Mr. Dwerrihouse had a key of his own."

"I never saw him, sir; I saw no one in that compartment but yourself. Beg pardon, sir, my time's up."

And with this the ruddy guard touched his cap and was gone. In another minute the heavy panting of the engine began afresh, and the train glided slowly out of the station.

We looked at each other for some moments in silence. I was the first to speak.

"Mr. Benjamin Somers knows more than he chooses to tell," I said.

"Humph! do you think so?"

"It must be. He could not have come to the door without seeing him. It's impossible."

"There is one thing not impossible, my dear fellow."

"What is that?"

"That you may have fallen asleep, and dreamt the whole thing."

"Could I dream of a branch line that I had never heard of? Could I dream of a hundred and one business details that had no kind of interest for me? Could I dream of the seventy-five thousand pounds?"

"Perhaps you might have seen, or heard, some vague account of the affair while you were abroad. It might have made no impression upon you at the time, and might have come back to you in your dreams—recalled, perhaps, by the mere names of the stations on the line."

"What about the fire in the chimney of the blue room—should I have heard of that during my journey?"

"Well, no; I admit there is a difficulty about that point."

"And what about the cigar-case?"

"Ay, by Jove! there is the cigar-case. That *is* a stubborn fact. Well, it's a mysterious affair, and it will need a better detective than myself, I fancy, to clear it up. I suppose we may as well go home."

Chapter III

A week had not gone by when I received a letter from the Secretary of the East Anglian Railway Company, requesting the favour of my attendance at a special board meeting, not then many days distant. No reasons were alleged, and no apologies offered, for this demand upon my time; but they had heard, it was clear, of my inquiries about the missing director, and had a mind to put me through some sort of official examination upon the subject. Being still a guest at Dumbleton Hall, I had to go up to London for the purpose, and Jonathan Jelf accompanied me. I found the direction of the Great East Anglian line represented by a party of some twelve or fourteen gentlemen seated in solemn conclave round a huge green-baize table in a gloomy board-room adjoining the London terminus.

Being courteously received by the chairman (who at once began by saying that certain statements of mine respecting Mr. John Dwerrihouse had come to the knowledge of the direction, and that they in consequence desired to confer with me on those points), we were placed at the table, and the inquiry proceeded in due form.

I was first asked if I knew Mr. John Dwerrihouse, how long I had been acquainted with him, and whether I could identify him at sight. I was then asked when I had seen him last. To which I replied, "On the fourth of this present month, December, eighteen hundred and fifty-six."

Then came the inquiry of where I had seen him on that fourth day of December; to which I replied that I met him in a first-class compartment of the 4.15 down-Express; that he got in just as the train was leaving the London terminus, and that he alighted at Blackwater station. The chairman then inquired whether I had held any communication with my fellow-traveller; whereupon I related, as nearly as I could remember it, the whole bulk and substance of Mr. John Dwerrihouse's diffuse information respecting the new branch line.

To all this the board listened with profound attention, while the chairman presided and the secretary took notes. I then produced the cigar-case. It was passed from hand to hand, and recognised by all. There was not a man present who did not remember that plain cigar-case with its silver monogram, or to whom it seemed anything less than entirely corroborative of my evidence.

When, at length, I had told all that I had to tell, the chairman whispered something to the secretary; the secretary touched a silver hand-bell; and the guard, Benjamin Somers, was ushered into the room. He was then examined as carefully as myself. He declared that he knew Mr. John Dwerrihouse perfectly well; that he could not be mistaken in him; that he remembered going down with the 4.15 Express on the afternoon in question; that he remembered me; and that, there being one or two empty first-class compartments on that especial afternoon, he had, in compliance with my request, placed me in a carriage by myself. He was positive that I remained alone in that compartment all the way from London to Clayborough. He was ready to take his oath that Mr. Dwerrihouse was neither in that carriage with me, nor in any compartment of that train. He remembered distinctly to have examined my ticket at Blackwater; was certain that there was no one else at that time in the carriage; could not have failed to observe a second person, if there had been one; had that second person been Mr. John Dwerrihouse, should have quietly double-locked the door of the carriage, and have given information to the Blackwater station-master. So clear, so decisive, so ready, was Somers with this testimony, that the board looked fairly puzzled.

"You hear this person's statement, Mr. Langford," said the chairman. "It contradicts yours in every particular. What have you to say in reply?"

"I can only repeat what I said before. I am quite as positive of the truth of my own assertions as Mr. Somers can be of the truth of his."

"You say that Mr. Dwerrihouse alighted at Blackwater, and that he was in possession of a private key. Are you sure that he had not alighted by means of that key before the guard came round for the tickets?"

"I am quite positive that he did not leave the carriage till the train had fairly entered the station and the other Blackwater passengers alighted. I even saw that he was met there by a friend."

"Indeed! Did you see that person distinctly?"

"Quite distinctly."

"Can you describe his appearance?"

"I think so. He was short and very slight, sandy-haired, with a bushy moustache and beard, and he wore a closely-fitting suit of grey tweed. His age I should take to be about thirty-eight or forty."

"Did Mr. Dwerrihouse leave the station in this person's company?"

"I cannot tell. I saw them walking together down the platform, and then I saw them standing aside under a gas-jet, talking earnestly. After that I lost sight of them quite suddenly; and just then my train went on, and I with it."

The chairman and secretary conferred together in an undertone. The directors whispered to each other. One or two looked suspiciously at the guard. I could see that my evidence remained unshaken, and that, like myself, they suspected some complicity between the guard and the defaulter.

"How far did you conduct that 4.15 Express on the day in question, Somers?" asked the chairman.

"All through, sir," replied the guard; "from London to Crampton."

"How was it that you were not relieved at Clayborough? I thought there was always a change of guards at Clayborough."

"There used to be, sir, till the new regulations came in force last Midsummer; since when, the guards in charge of Express trains go the whole way through."

The chairman turned to the secretary.

"I think it would be as well," he said, "if we had the day-book to refer to upon this point."

Again the secretary touched the silver hand-bell, and desired the porter in attendance to summon Mr. Raikes. From a word or two dropped by another of the directors, I gathered that Mr. Raikes was one of the under-secretaries.

He came—a small, slight, sandy-haired, keen-eyed man, with an eager, nervous manner, and a forest of light beard and moustache. He just showed himself at the door of the board-room, and being requested to bring a certain day-book from a certain shelf in a certain room, bowed and vanished.

He was there such a moment, and the surprise of seeing him was so great and sudden, that it was not till the door had closed upon him that I found voice to speak. He was no sooner gone, however, than I sprang to my feet.

"That person," I said, "is the same who met Mr. Dwerrihouse upon the platform at Blackwater!"

There was a general movement of surprise. The chairman looked grave, and somewhat agitated.

"Take care, Mr. Langford," he said, "take care what you say!"

"I am as positive of his identity as of my own."

"Do you consider the consequences of your words? Do you consider that you are bringing a charge of the gravest character against one of the company's servants?"

"I am willing to be put upon my oath, if necessary. The man who came to that door a minute since is the same whom I saw talking with Mr. Dwerrihouse on the Blackwater platform. Were he twenty times the company's servant, I could say neither more nor less."

The chairman turned again to the guard.

"Did you see Mr. Raikes in the train, or on the platform?" he asked.

Somers shook his head.

"I am confident Mr. Raikes was not in the train," he said; "and I certainly did not see him on the platform."

The chairman turned next to the secretary.

"Mr. Raikes is in your office, Mr. Hunter," he said. "Can you remember if he was absent on the fourth instant?"

"I do not think he was," replied the secretary; "but I am not prepared to speak positively. I have been away most afternoons myself lately, and Mr. Raikes might easily have absented himself if he had been disposed."

At this moment the under-secretary returned with the day-book under his arm.

"Be pleased to refer, Mr. Raikes," said the chairman, "to the entries of the fourth instant, and see what Benjamin Somers' duties were on that day."

Mr. Raikes threw open the cumbrous volume, and ran a practised eye and finger down some three or four successive columns of entries. Stopping suddenly at the foot of a page, he then read aloud that Benjamin Somers had on that day conducted the 4.15 Express from London to Crampton.

The chairman leaned forward in his seat, looked the under-secretary full in the face, and said, quite sharply and suddenly:—

"Where were *you*, Mr. Raikes, on the same afternoon?"

"*I*, sir?"

"You, Mr. Raikes. Where were you on the afternoon and evening of the fourth of the present month?"

"Here, sir—in Mr. Hunter's office. Where else should I be?"

There was a dash of trepidation in the under-secretary's voice as he said this; but his look of surprise was natural enough.

"We have some reason for believing, Mr. Raikes, that you were absent that afternoon without leave. Was this the case?"

"Certainly not, sir. I have not had a day's holiday since September. Mr. Hunter will bear me out in this."

Mr. Hunter repeated what he had previously said on the subject, but added that the clerks in the adjoining office would be certain to know. Whereupon the senior clerk, a grave, middle-aged person, in green glasses, was summoned and interrogated.

His testimony cleared the under-secretary at once. He declared that Mr. Raikes had in no instance, to his knowledge, been absent during office hours since his return from his annual holiday in September.

I was confounded.

The chairman turned to me with a smile, in which a shade of covert annoyance was scarcely apparent.

"You hear, Mr. Langford?" he said.

"I hear, sir; but my conviction remains unshaken."

"I fear, Mr. Langford, that your convictions are very insufficiently based," replied the chairman, with a doubtful cough. "I fear that you 'dream dreams,' and mistake them for actual occurrences. It is a dangerous habit of mind, and might lead to dangerous results. Mr. Raikes here would have found himself in an unpleasant position, had he not proved so satisfactory an *alibi*."

I was about to reply, but he gave me no time.

"I think, gentlemen," he went on to say, addressing the board, "that we should be wasting time to push this inquiry further. Mr. Langford's evidence would seem to be of an equal value throughout. The testimony of Benjamin Somers disproves his first statement, and the testimony of the last witness disproves his second. I think we may conclude that Mr. Langford fell asleep in the train on the occasion of his journey to Clayborough, and dreamt an unusually vivid and circumstantial dream—of which, however, we have now heard quite enough."

There are few things more annoying than to find one's positive convictions met with incredulity. I could not help feeling impatience at the turn that affairs had taken. I was not proof against the civil sarcasm of the chairman's manner. Most intolerable of all, however, was the quiet smile lurking about the corners of Benjamin Somers' mouth, and the half-triumphant, half-malicious gleam in the eyes of the under-secretary. The man was evidently puzzled, and somewhat alarmed. His looks seemed furtively to interrogate me. Who was I? What did I want? Why had I come there to do him an ill turn with his employers? What was it to me whether or not he was absent without leave?

Seeing all this, and perhaps more irritated by it than the thing deserved, I begged leave to detain the attention of the board for a moment longer. Jelf plucked me impatiently by the sleeve.

"Better let the thing drop," he whispered. "The chairman's right enough. You dreamt it; and the less said now, the better."

I was not to be silenced, however, in this fashion. I had yet something to say, and I would say it. It was to this effect:—That dreams were not usually productive of tangible results, and that I requested to know in what way the chairman conceived I had evolved from my dream so substantial and well-made a delusion as the cigar-case which I had had the honour to place before him at the commencement of our interview.

"The cigar-case, I admit, Mr. Langford," the chairman replied, "is a very strong point in your evidence. It is your *only* strong point, however, and there is just a possibility that we may all be misled by a mere accidental resemblance. Will you permit me to see the case again?"

"It is unlikely," I said, as I handed it to him, "that any other should bear precisely this monogram, and also be in all other particulars exactly similar."

The chairman examined it for a moment in silence, and then passed it to Mr. Hunter. Mr. Hunter turned it over and over, and shook his head.

"This is no mere resemblance," he said. "It is John Dwerrihouse's cigar-case to a certainty. I remember it perfectly. I have seen it a hundred times."

"I believe I may say the same," added the chairman. "Yet how shall we account for the way in which Mr. Langford asserts that it came into his possession?"

"I can only repeat," I replied, "that I found it on the floor of the carriage after Mr. Dwerrihouse had alighted. It was in leaning out to look after him that I trod upon it; and it was in running after him for the purpose of restoring it that I saw—or believed I saw—Mr. Raikes standing aside with him in earnest conversation."

Again I felt Jonathan Jelf plucking at my sleeve.

"Look at Raikes," he whispered. "Look at Raikes!"

I turned to where the under-secretary had been standing a moment before, and saw him, white as death, with lips trembling and livid, stealing towards the door.

To conceive a sudden, strange, and indefinite suspicion; to fling myself in his way; to take him by the shoulders as if he were a child, and turn his craven face, perforce, towards the board, were with me the work of an instant.

"Look at him!" I exclaimed. "Look at his face! I ask no better witness to the truth of my words."

The chairman's brow darkened.

"Mr. Raikes," he said, sternly, "if you know anything, you had better speak."

Vainly trying to wrench himself from my grasp, the under-secretary stammered out an incoherent denial.

"Let me go!" he said. "I know nothing—you have no right to detain me—let me go!"

"Did you, or did you not, meet Mr. John Dwerrihouse at Blackwater station? The charge brought against you is either true or false. If true, you will do well to throw yourself upon the mercy of the board, and make full confession of all that you know."

The under-secretary wrung his hands in an agony of helpless terror.

"I was away," he cried. "I was two hundred miles away at the time! I know nothing about it—I have nothing to confess—I am innocent—I call God to witness I am innocent!"

"Two hundred miles away!" echoed the chairman. "What do you mean?"

"I was in Devonshire. I had three weeks' leave of absence—I appeal to Mr. Hunter—Mr. Hunter knows I had three weeks' leave of absence! I was in Devonshire all the time—I can prove I was in Devonshire!"

Seeing him so abject, so incoherent, so wild with apprehension, the directors began to whisper gravely among themselves; while one got quietly up, and called the porter to guard the door.

"What has your being in Devonshire to do with the matter?" said the chairman. "When were you in Devonshire?"

"Mr. Raikes took his leave in September," said the secretary; "about the time when Mr. Dwerrihouse disappeared."

"I never even heard that he had disappeared till I came back!"

"That must remain to be proved," said the chairman. "I shall at once put this matter in the hands of the police. In the meanwhile, Mr. Raikes, being myself a magistrate, and used to deal with these cases, I advise you to offer no resistance; but to confess while confession may yet do you service. As for your accomplice...."

The frightened wretch fell upon his knees.

"I had no accomplice!" he cried. "Only have mercy upon me—only spare my life, and I will confess all! I didn't mean to harm him—I didn't mean to hurt a hair of his head. Only have mercy upon me, and let me go!"

The chairman rose in his place, pale and agitated. "Good heavens!" he exclaimed, "what horrible mystery is this? What does it mean?"

"As sure as there is a God in heaven," said Jonathan Jelf, "it means that murder has been done."

"No—no—no!" shrieked Raikes, still upon his knees, and cowering like a beaten hound. "Not murder! No jury that ever sat could bring it in murder. I thought I had only stunned him—I never meant to do more than stun him! Manslaughter—manslaughter—not murder!"

Overcome by the horror of this unexpected revelation, the chairman covered his face with his hand, and for a moment or two remained silent.

"Miserable man," he said at length, "you have betrayed yourself."

"You bade me confess! You urged me to throw myself upon the mercy of the board!"

"You have confessed to a crime which no one suspected you of having committed," replied the chairman, "and which this board has no power either to punish or forgive. All that I can do for you is to advise you to submit to the law, to plead guilty, and to conceal nothing. When did you do this deed?"

The guilty man rose to his feet, and leaned heavily against the table. His answer came reluctantly, like the speech of one dreaming.

"On the twenty-second of September!"

On the twenty-second of September! I looked in Jonathan Jelf's face, and he in mine. I felt my own paling with a strange sense of wonder and dread. I saw his blench suddenly, even to the lips.

"Merciful heaven!" he whispered, "*what was It, then, that you saw in the train?*"

What was it that I saw in the train? That question remains unanswered to this day. I have never been able to reply to it. I only know that it bore the living likeness of the murdered man, whose body had been lying some ten weeks under a rough pile of branches, and brambles, and rotting leaves, at the bottom of a deserted chalk-pit about half way between Blackwater and Mallingford. I know that it spoke, and moved, and looked as that man spoke, and moved, and looked in life; that I heard, or seemed to hear, things related which I could never otherwise have learned; that I was guided, as it were, by that vision on the platform to the identification of the murderer; and that, a passive instrument myself, I was destined, by means of these mysterious teachings, to bring about the ends of justice. For these things I have never been able to account.

As for that matter of the cigar-case, it proved, on inquiry, that the carriage in which I travelled down that afternoon to Clayborough had not been in use for several weeks, and was, in point of fact, the same in which poor John Dwerrihouse had performed his last journey. The case had, doubtless, been dropped by him, and had lain unnoticed till I found it.

Upon the details of the murder I have no need to dwell. Those who desire more ample particulars may find them, and the written confession of Augustus Raikes, in the files of the "Times" for 1856. Enough that the under-secretary, knowing the history of the new line, and following the negotiation step by step through all its stages, determined to waylay Mr. Dwerrihouse, rob him of the seventy-five thousand pounds, and escape to America with his booty.

In order to effect these ends he obtained leave of absence a few days before the time appointed for the payment of the money; secured his passage across the Atlantic in a steamer advertised to start on the twenty-third; provided himself with a heavily loaded "life-preserver," and went down to Blackwater to await the arrival of his victim. How he met him on the platform with a pretended message from the board; how he offered to conduct him by a short cut across the fields to Mallingford; how, having brought him to a lonely place, he struck him down with the life-preserver, and so killed him; and how, finding what he had done, he dragged the body to the verge of an out-of-the-way chalk-pit, and there flung it in, and piled it over with branches and brambles, are facts still fresh in the memories of those who, like the connoisseurs in De Quincey's famous essay, regard murder as a fine art. Strangely enough, the murderer, having done his work, was afraid to leave the country. He declared that he had not intended to take the director's life, but only to stun and rob him; and that, finding the blow had killed, he dared not fly for fear of drawing down suspicion upon his own head. As a mere robber he would have been safe in the States, but as a murderer he would inevitably have been pursued, and given up to justice. So he forfeited his passage, returned to the office as usual at the end of his leave, and locked up his ill-gotten thousands till a more convenient opportunity. In the meanwhile he had the satisfaction of finding that Mr. Dwerrihouse was universally believed to have absconded with the money, no one knew how or whither.

Whether he meant murder or not, however, Mr. Augustus Raikes paid the full penalty of his crime, and was hanged at the Old Bailey in the second week in January, 1857. Those who desire to make his further acquaintance may see him any day (admirably done in wax) in the Chamber of Horrors at Madame Tussaud's exhibition, in Baker Street. He is there to be found in the midst of a select society of ladies and gentlemen of atrocious memory, dressed in the close-cut tweed suit which he wore on the evening of the murder, and holding in his hand the identical life-preserver with which he committed it.

SINCE I DIED*

Elizabeth Stuart Phelps

How very still you sit!

If the shadow of an eyelash stirred upon your cheek; if that gray line about your mouth should snap its tension at this quivering end; if the pallor of your profile warmed a little; if that tiny muscle on your forehead, just at the left eyebrow's curve, should start and twitch; if you would but grow a trifle restless, sitting there beneath my steady gaze; if you moved a finger of your folded hands; if you should turn and look behind your chair, or lift your face, half lingering and half longing, half loving and half loth, to ponder on the annoyed and thwarted cry which the wind is making, where I stand between it and yourself, against the half-closed window— Ah, there! You sigh and stir, I think. You lift your head. The little muscle is a captive still; the line about your mouth is tense and hard; the deepening hollow in your cheek has no warmer tint, I see, than the great Doric column which the moonlight builds against the wall. I lean against it; I hold out my arms.

You lift your head and look me in the eye.

If a shudder crept across your figure; if your arms, laid out upon the table, leaped but once above your head; if you named my name; if you held your breath with terror, or sobbed aloud for love, or sprang, or cried—

But you only lift your head and look me in the eye.

If I dared step near, or nearer; if it were Permitted that I should cross the current of your living breath; if it were Willed that I should feel the leap of human blood within your veins; if I should touch your hands, your cheeks, your lips; if I dropped an arm as lightly as a snow-flake round your shoulder—

The fear which no heart has fathomed, the fate which no fancy has faced, the riddle which no soul has read, steps between your substance and my soul.

I drop my arms. I sink into the heart of the pillared light upon the wall. I will

* "Since I Died" was originally published in the February 1873 issue of *Scribner's Monthly* and was later included in Phelps's collection *Sealed Orders* (Boston: Houghton, Osgood, 1879). The current text is based on the 1879 edition. Obvious typographical errors and inconsistencies have been silently corrected.

not wonder what would happen if my outline were defined upon it to your view. I will not think of that which could be, would be, if I struck across your vision, face to face.

Ah me, how still she sits! With what a fixed, incurious stare she looks me in the eye!

The wind, now that I stand no longer between it and yourself, comes enviously in. It lifts the curtain, and whirls about the room. It bruises the surface of the great pearled pillar where I lean. I am caught within it. Speech and language struggle over me. Mute articulations fill the air.

Tears and laughter, and the sounding of soft lips, and the falling of low cries, possess me. Will she listen? Will she bend her head? Will her lips part in recognition? Is there an alphabet between us? Or have the winds of night a vocabulary to lift before her holden eyes?

We sat many times together, and talked of this. Do you remember, dear? You held my hand. Tears that I could not see, fell on it; we sat by the great hall-window up-stairs, where the maple shadow goes to sleep, face down across the floor, upon a lighted night; the old green curtain waved its hands upon us like a mesmerist, I thought; like a priest, you said.

"When we are parted, you shall go," you said; and when I shook my head you smiled—you always smiled when you said that, but you said it always quite the same.

I think I hardly understood you then. Now that I hold your eyes in mine, and you see me not; now when I stretch my hand and you touch me not; now that I cry your name, and you hear it not,—I comprehend you, tender one! A wisdom not of earth was in your words. "To live, is dying; I will die. To die is life, and you shall live."

Now when the fever turned, I thought of this.

That must have been—ah! how long ago? I miss the conception of that for which *how long* stands index.

Yet I perfectly remember that I perfectly understood it to be at three o'clock on a rainy Sunday morning that I died. Your little watch stood in its case of olive-wood upon the table, and drops were on the window. I noticed both, though you did not know it. I see the watch now, in your pocket; I cannot tell if the hands move, or only pulsate like a heart-throb, to and fro; they stand and point, mute golden fingers, paralyzed and pleading, forever at the hour of three. At this I wonder.

When first you said I "was sinking fast," the words sounded as old and familiar as a nursery tale. I heard you in the hall. The doctor had just left, and you went to mother and took her face in your two arms, and laid your hand across her mouth, as if it were she who had spoken. She cried out and threw up her thin old hands; but you stood as still as Eternity. Then I thought again: "It is she who dies; I shall live."

So often and so anxiously we have talked of this thing called death, that now that it is all over between us, I cannot understand why we found in it such a source of distress. It bewilders me. I am often bewildered here. Things and the fancies of things possess a relation which as yet is new and strange to me. Here is a mystery.

Now, in truth, it seems a simple matter for me to tell you how it has been with me since your lips last touched me, and your arms held me to the vanishing air.

Oh, drawn, pale lips! Nerveless, dropping arms! I told you I would come. Did ever promise fail I spoke to you? "Come and show me Death," you said. I have come to show you Death. I could show you the fairest sight and sweetest, that ever blessed your eyes. Why, look! Is it not fair? Am I terrible? Do you shrink or shiver? Would you turn from me, or hide your strained, expectant face?

Would she? Does she? Will she?—

Ah, how the room widened! I could tell you that. It grew great and luminous day by day. At night the walls throbbed; lights of rose ran round them, and blue fire, and a tracery as of the shadows of little leaves. As the walls expanded, the air fled. But I tried to tell you how little pain I knew or feared. Your haggard face bent over me. I could not speak; when I would, I struggled, and you said "She suffers!" Dear, it was so very little!

Listen, till I tell you how that night came on. The sun fell, and the dew slid down. It seemed to me that it slid into my heart, but still I felt no pain. Where the walls pulsed and receded, the hills came in. Where the old bureau stood, above the glass, I saw a single mountain with a face of fire, and purple hair. I tried to tell you this, but you said: "She wanders." I laughed in my heart at that, for it was such a blessed wandering! As the night locked the sun below the mountain's solemn, watching face, the Gates of Space were lifted up before me; the everlasting doors of Matter swung for me upon their rusty hinges, and the King of Glories entered in and out. All the kingdoms of the earth, and the power of them, beckoned to me, across the mist my failing senses made,—ruins and roses, and the brows of Jura and the singing of the Rhine; a shaft of red light on the Sphinx's smile, and caravans in sand-storms, and an icy wind at sea, and gold in mines that no man knew, and mothers sitting at their doors in valleys singing babes to sleep, and women in dank cellars selling souls for bread, and the whir of wheels in giant factories, and a single prayer somewhere in a den of death,—I could not find it, though I searched,—and the smoke of battle, and broken music, and a sense of lilies alone beside a stream at the rising of the sun—and, at last, your face, dear, all alone.

I discovered then, that the walls and roof of the room had vanished quite. The night-wind blew in. The maple in the yard almost brushed my cheek. Stars were about me, and I thought the rain had stopped, yet seemed to hear it, upon the seeming of a window which I could not find.

One thing only hung between me and immensity. It was your single, awful, haggard face. I looked my last into your eyes. Stronger than death, they held and claimed my soul. I feebly raised my hand to find your own. More cruel than the grave, your wild grasp chained me. Then I struggled, and you cried out, and your face slipped, and I stood free.

I stood upon the floor, beside the bed. That which had been I, lay there at rest, but terrible, before me. You hid your face, and I saw you slide upon your knees. I laid my hand upon your head; you did not stir; I spoke to you: "Dear, look around a minute!" but you knelt quite still. I walked to and fro about the room, and meeting my mother, touched her on the elbow; she only said, "She's gone!" and sobbed aloud. "I have not *gone!*" I cried; but she sat sobbing on.

The walls of the room had settled now, and the ceiling stood in its solid place. The window was shut, but the door stood open. Suddenly I was restless, and I ran.

I brushed you in hurrying by, and hit the little light-stand where the tumblers stood; I looked to see if it would fall, but it only shivered as if a breath of wind had struck it once.

But I was restless, and I ran. In the hall I met the doctor. This amused me, and I stopped to think it over. "Ah, Doctor," said I, "you need not trouble yourself to go up. I'm quite well to-night, you see." But he made me no answer; he gave me no glance; he hung up his hat, and laid his hand upon the banister against which I leaned, and went ponderously up.

It was not until he had nearly reached the landing that it occurred to me, still leaning on the banister, that his heavy arm must have swept against and *through* me, where I stood against the oaken moldings which he grasped.

I saw his feet fall on the stairs above me; but they made no sound which reached my ear. "You'll not disturb me *now* with your big boots, sir," said I, nodding; "never fear!"

But he disappeared from sight above me, and still I heard no sound.

Now the doctor had left the front door unlatched.

As I touched it, it blew open wide, and solemnly. I passed out and down the steps. I could see that it was chilly, yet I felt no chill. Frost was on the grass, and in the east a pallid streak, like the cheek of one who had watched all night. The flowers in the little square plots hung their heads and drew their shoulders up; there was a lonely, late lily which I broke and gathered to my heart, where I breathed upon it, and it warmed and looked me kindly in the eye. This, I remember, gave me pleasure. I wandered in and out about the garden in the scattering rain; my feet left no trace upon the dripping grass, and I saw with interest that the garment which I wore, gathered no moisture and no cold. I sat musing for a while upon the piazza, in the garden-chair, not caring to go in. It was so many months since I had felt able to sit upon the piazza in the open air. "By and by," I thought, I would go in and up-stairs to see you once again. The curtains were drawn from the parlor windows and I passed and repassed, looking in.

All this while the cheek of the east was warming, and the air gathering faint heats and lights about me. I remembered, presently, the old arbor at the garden-foot, where, before I was sick, we sat so much together; and thinking, "She will be surprised to know that I have been down alone," I was restless, and I ran again.

I meant to come back and see you, dear, once more. I saw the lights in the room where I had lain sick, overhead; and your shadow on the curtain; and I blessed it with all the love of life and death, as I bounded by.

The air was thick with sweetness from the dying flowers. The birds woke, and the zenith lighted, and the leap of health was in my limbs. The old arbor held out its soft arms to me—but I was restless, and I ran.

The field opened before me, and meadows with broad bosoms, and a river flashed before me like a scimitar, and woods interlocked their hands to stay me—but being restless, on I ran.

The house dwindled behind me; and the light in my sick-room, and your shadow on the curtain. But yet I was restless, and I ran.

In the twinkling of an eye I fell into a solitary place. Sand and rocks were in it, and a falling wind. I paused, and knelt upon the sand, and mused a little in this place. I mused of you, and life and death, and love and agony;—but these had departed from me, as dim and distant as the fainting wind. A sense of solemn expectation filled the air. A tremor and a trouble wrapped my soul.

"I must be dead!" I said aloud. I had no sooner spoken than I learned that I was not alone.

The sun had risen, and on a ledge of ancient rock, weather-stained and red, there had fallen over against me the outline of a Presence lifted up against the sky; and turning suddenly, I saw....

Lawful to utter, but utterance has fled! Lawful to utter, but a greater than Law restrains me! Am I blotted from your desolate fixed eyes? Lips that my mortal lips have pressed, can you not quiver when I cry? Soul that my eternal soul has loved, can you stand enveloped in my presence, and not spring like a fountain to me? Would you not know how it has been with me since your perishable eyes beheld my perished face? What my eyes have seen, or my ears have heard, or my heart conceived without you? If I have missed or mourned for you? If I have watched or longed for you? Marked your solitary days and sleepless nights, and tearless eyes, and monotonous slow echo of my unanswering name? Would you not know?

"Alas! would she? Would she not? My soul misgives me with a matchless, solitary fear. I am called, and I slip from her. I am beckoned, and I lose her.

Her face dims, and her folded, lonely hands fade from my sight.

Time to tell her a guarded thing! Time to whisper a treasured word! A moment to tell her that *Death is dumb, for Life is deaf!* A moment to tell her—

THE SHADOW IN THE CORNER*
Mary Elizabeth Braddon

Wildheath Grange stood a little way back from the road, with a barren stretch of heath behind it, and a few tall fir-trees, with straggling wind-tossed heads, for its only shelter. It was a lonely house on a lonely road, little better than a lane, leading across a desolate waste of sandy fields to the sea-shore; and it was a house that bore a bad name among the natives of the village of Holcroft, which was the nearest place where humanity might be found.

It was a good old house, nevertheless, substantially built in the days when there was no stint of stone and timber—a good old grey stone house, with many gables, deep window seats, and a wide staircase, long dark passages, hidden doors in queer corners, closets as large as some modern rooms, and cellars in which a company of soldiers might have lain perdu.

This spacious old mansion was given over to rats and mice, loneliness, echoes, and the occupation of three elderly people; Michael Bascom, whose forbears had been landowners of importance in the neighbourhood, and his two servants, Daniel Skegg and his wife, who had served the owner of that grim old house ever since he left the university, where he had lived fifteen years of his life—five as student, and ten as professor of natural science.

At three-and-thirty Michael Bascom had seemed a middle-aged man; at fifty-six he looked and moved and spoke like on old man. During that interval of twenty-three years he had lived alone in Wildheath Grange, and the country people told each other that the house had made him what he was. This was a fanciful and superstitious notion on their part, doubtless; yet it would not have been difficult to have traced a certain affinity between the dull grey building and the man who lived in it. Both seemed alike remote from the common cares and interests of humanity; both had an air of settled melancholy, engendered by perpetual solitude; both had

---

* "The Shadow in the Corner" first appeared in the Extra Summer Number of *All the Year Round* in 1879 and was later collected in Braddon's *Flower and Weed and Other Tales* (London: John and Robert Maxwell, [1883]). The current text is based on the 1883 edition. Obvious typographical errors and inconsistencies have been silently corrected.

the same faded complexion, the same look of slow decay.

Yet lonely as Michael Bascom's life was at Wildheath Grange, he would not for any consideration have altered its tenor. He had been glad to exchange the comparative seclusion of college rooms for the unbroken solitude of Wildheath. He was a fanatic in his love of scientific research, and his quiet days were filled to the brim with labours that seldom failed to interest and satisfy him. There were periods of depression, occasional hours of doubt, when the goal towards which he strove seemed unattainable, and his spirit fainted within him. Happily such times were rare with him. He had a dogged power of continuity which ought to have carried him to the highest pinnacle of achievement, and which perhaps might ultimately have won for him a grand name and a world-wide renown, but for a catastrophe which burdened the declining years of his harmless life with an unconquerable remorse.

One autumn morning—when he had lived just three-and-twenty years at Wildheath, and had only lately begun to perceive that his faithful butler and body servant, who was middle-aged when he first employed him, was actually getting old—Mr. Bascom's breakfast meditations over the latest treatise on the atomic theory were interrupted by an abrupt demand from that very Daniel Skegg. The man was accustomed to wait upon his master in the most absolute silence, and his sudden breaking out into speech was almost as startling as if the bust of Socrates above the bookcase had burst into human language.

"It's no use," said Daniel; "my missus must have a girl!"

"A what?" demanded Mr. Bascom, without taking his eyes from this line he had been reading.

"A girl—a girl to trot about and wash up, and help the old lady. She's getting weak on her legs, poor soul. We've none of us grown younger in the last twenty years."

"Twenty years!" echoed Michael Bascom scornfully. "What is twenty years in the formation of a stratum—what even in the growth of an oak—the cooling of a volcano!"

"Not much, perhaps, but it's apt to tell upon the bones of a human being."

"The manganese staining to be seen upon some skulls would certainly indicate——" began the scientist dreamily.

"I wish my bones were only as free from rheumatics as they were twenty years ago," pursued Daniel testily; "and then perhaps *I* should make light of twenty years. Howsoever, the long and the short of it is, my missus must have a girl. She can't go on trotting up and down these everlasting passages, and standing in that stony scullery year after year, just as if she was a young woman. She must have a girl to help."

"Let her have twenty girls," said Mr. Bascom, going back to his book.

"What's the use of talking like that, sir? Twenty girls, indeed! We shall have rare work to get one."

"Because the neighbourhood is sparsely populated?" interrogated Mr. Bascom, still reading.

"No, sir. Because this house is known to be haunted."

Michael Bascom laid down his book, and turned a look of grave reproach upon his servant.

"Skegg," he said in a severe voice, "I thought you had lived long enough with me to be superior to any folly of that kind."

"I don't say that *I* believe in ghosts," answered Daniel with a semi-apologetic air; "but the country people do. There's not a mortal among 'em that will venture across our threshold after nightfall."

"Merely because Anthony Bascom, who led a wild life in London, and lost his money and land, came home here broken-hearted, and is supposed to have destroyed himself in this house—the only remnant of property that was left him out of a fine estate."

"Supposed to have destroyed himself!" cried Skegg; "why the fact is as well known as the death of Queen Elizabeth, or the great fire of London. Why, wasn't he buried at the cross-roads between here and Holcroft?"

"An idle tradition, for which you could produce no substantial proof," retorted Mr. Bascom.

"I don't know about proof; but the country people believe it as firmly as they believe their Gospel."

"If their faith in the Gospel was a little stronger they need not trouble themselves about Anthony Bascom."

"Well," grumbled Daniel, as he began to clear the table, "a girl of some kind we must get, but she'll have to be a foreigner, or a girl that's hard driven for a place."

When Daniel Skegg said a foreigner, he did not mean the native of some distant land, but a girl who had not been born and bred at Holcroft. Daniel had been raised and reared in that insignificant hamlet, and, small and dull as the spot was, he considered it the centre of the earth, and the world beyond it only margin.

Michael Bascom was too deep in the atomic theory to give a second thought to the necessities of an old servant. Mrs. Skegg was an individual with whom he rarely came in contact. She lived for the most part in a gloomy region at the north end of the house, where she ruled over the solitude of a kitchen, that looked almost as big as a cathedral, and numerous offices of the scullery, larder, and pantry class, where she carried on a perpetual warfare with spiders and beetles, and wore her old life out in the labour of sweeping and scrubbing. She was a woman of severe aspect, dogmatic piety, and a bitter tongue. She was a good plain cook, and ministered diligently to her master's wants. He was not an epicure, but liked his life to be smooth and easy, and the equilibrium of his mental power would have been disturbed by a bad dinner.

He heard no more about the proposed addition to his household for a space of ten days, when Daniel Skegg again startled him amidst his studious repose by the abrupt announcement—

"I've got a girl!"

"Oh," said Michael Bascom; "have you?" and he went on with his book.

This time he was reading an essay on phosphorus and its functions in relation to the human brain.

"Yes," pursued Daniel in his usual grumbling tone; "she was a waif and stray, or I shouldn't have got her. If she'd been a native she'd never have come to us."

"I hope she's respectable," said Michael.

"Respectable! That's the only fault she has, poor thing. She's too good for the place. She's never been in service before, but she says she's willing to work, and I daresay my old woman will be able to break her in. Her father was a small tradesman at Yarmouth. He died a month ago, and left this poor thing homeless. Mrs. Midge, at Holcroft, is her aunt, and she said to the girl, come and stay with me till you get a place; and the girl has been staying with Mrs. Midge for the last three weeks, trying to hear of a place. When Mrs. Midge heard that my missus wanted a girl to help, she thought it would be the very thing for her niece Maria. Luckily Maria had heard nothing about this house, so the poor innocent dropped me a curtsey, and said she'd be thankful to come, and would do her best to learn her duty. She'd had an easy time of it with her father, who had educated her above her station, like a fool as he was," growled Daniel.

"By your own account I'm afraid you've made a bad bargain," said Michael. "You don't want a young lady to clean kettles and pans."

"If she was a young duchess my old woman would make her work," retorted Skegg decisively.

"And pray where are you going to put this girl?" asked Mr. Bascom, rather irritably; "I can't have a strange young woman tramping up and down the passages outside my room. You know what a wretched sleeper I am, Skegg. A mouse behind the wainscot is enough to wake me."

"I've thought of that," answered the butler, with his look of ineffable wisdom. "I'm not going to put her on your floor. She's to sleep in the attics."

"Which room?"

"The big one at the north end of the house. That's the only ceiling that doesn't let water. She might as well sleep in a shower-bath as in any of the other attics."

"The room at the north end," repeated Mr. Bascom thoughtfully; "isn't that——?"

"Of course it is," snapped Skegg; "but she doesn't know anything about it."

Mr. Bascom went back to his books, and forgot all about the orphan from Yarmouth, until one morning on entering his study he was startled by the appearance of a strange girl, in a neat black and white cotton gown, busy dusting the volumes which were stacked in blocks upon his spacious writing-table—and doing it with such deft and careful hands that he had no inclination to be angry at this unwonted liberty. Old Mrs. Skegg had religiously refrained from all such dusting, on the plea that she did not wish to interfere with the master's ways. One of the master's ways, therefore, had been to inhale a good deal of dust in the course of his studies.

The girl was a slim little thing, with a pale and somewhat old-fashioned face, flaxen hair, braided under a neat muslin cap, a very fair complexion, and light blue eyes. They were the lightest blue eyes Michael Bascom had ever seen, but there was a sweetness and gentleness in their expression which atoned for their insipid colour.

"I hope you do not object to my dusting your books, sir," she said, dropping a curtsey.

She spoke with a quaint precision which struck Michael Bascom as a pretty thing in its way.

"No; I don't object to cleanliness, so long as my books and papers are not disturbed. If you take a volume off my desk, replace it on the spot you took it from. That's all I ask."

"I will be very careful, sir."

"When did you come here?"

"Only this morning, sir."

The student seated himself at his desk, and the girl withdrew, drifting out of the room as noiselessly as a flower blown across the threshold. Michael Bascom looked after her curiously. He had seen very little of youthful womanhood in his dry-as-dust career, and he wondered at this girl as at a creature of a species hitherto unknown to him. How fairly and delicately she was fashioned; what a translucent skin; what soft and pleasing accents issued from those rose- tinted lips. A pretty thing, assuredly, this kitchen wench! A pity that in all this busy world there could be no better work found for her than the scouring of pots and pans.

Absorbed in considerations about dry bones, Mr. Bascom thought no more of the pale-faced handmaiden. He saw her no more about his rooms. Whatever work she did there was done early in the morning, before the scholar's breakfast.

She had been a week in the house, when he met her one day in the hall. He was struck by the change in her appearance.

The girlish lips had lost their rose-bud hue; the pale blue eyes had a frightened look, and there were dark rings round them, as in one whose nights had been sleepless, or troubled by evil dreams.

Michael Bascom was so startled by an undefinable look in the girl's face that, reserved as he was by habit and nature, he expanded so far as to ask her what ailed her.

"There is something amiss, I am sure," he said. "What is it?"

"Nothing, sir," she faltered, looking still more scared at his question. "Indeed, it is nothing; or nothing worth troubling you about."

"Nonsense. Do you suppose, because I live among books, I have no sympathy with my fellow-creatures? Tell me what is wrong with you, child. You have been grieving about the father you have lately lost, I suppose."

"No, sir; it is not that. I shall never leave off being sorry for that. It is a grief which will last me all my life."

"What, there is something else then?" asked Michael impatiently. "I see; you are not happy here. Hard work does not suit you. I thought as much."

"Oh, sir, please don't think that," cried the girl, very earnestly. "Indeed I am glad to work—glad to be in service; it is only——"

She faltered and broke down, the tears rolling slowly from her sorrowful eyes, despite her effort to keep them back.

"Only what?" cried Michael, growing angry. "The girl is full of secrets and mysteries. What do you mean, wench?"

"I—I know it is very foolish, sir; but I am afraid of the room where I sleep."

"Afraid! Why?"

"Shall I tell you the truth, sir? Will you promise not to be angry?"

"I will not be angry if you will only speak plainly; but you provoke me by these hesitations and suppressions."

"And please, sir, do not tell Mrs. Skegg that I have told you. She would scold me, or perhaps even send me away."

"Mrs. Skegg shall not scold you. Go on, child."

"You may not know the room where I sleep, sir; it is a large room at one end of the house, looking towards the sea. I can see the dark line of water from the window, and I wonder sometimes to think that it is the same ocean I used to see when I was a child at Yarmouth. It is very lonely, sir, at the top of the house. Mr. and Mrs. Skegg sleep in a little room near the kitchen, you know, sir, and I am quite alone on the top floor."

"Skegg told me you had been educated in advance of your position in life, Maria. I should have thought the first effect of a good education would have been to make you superior to any foolish fancies about empty rooms."

"Oh, pray sir, do not think it is any fault in my education. Father took such pains with me; he spared no expense in giving me as good an education as a tradesman's daughter need wish for. And he was a religious man, sir. He did not believe"—here she paused with a suppressed shudder—"in the spirits of the dead appearing to the living since the days of miracles, when the ghost of Samuel appeared to Saul. He never put any foolish ideas into my head, sir. I hadn't a thought of fear when I first lay down to rest in the big lonely room upstairs."

"Well, what then?"

"But on the very first night," the girl went on breathlessly, "I felt weighed down in my sleep as if there were some heavy burden laid upon my chest. It was not a bad dream, but it was a sense of trouble that followed me all through my sleep; and just at daybreak—it begins to be light a little after six—I woke suddenly, with the cold perspiration pouring down my face, and knew that there was something dreadful in the room."

"What do you mean by something dreadful. Did you see anything?"

"Not much, sir; but it froze the blood in my veins, and I knew it was this that had been following me and weighing upon me all through my sleep. In the corner between the fire-place and the wardrobe, I saw a shadow—a dim, shapeless shadow——"

"Produced by an angle of the wardrobe, I daresay."

"No, sir. I could see the shadow of the wardrobe, distinct and sharp, as if it had been painted on the wall. This shadow was in the corner—a strange, shapeless mass; or, if it had any shape at all, it seemed——"

"What?" asked Michael eagerly.

"The shape of a dead body hanging against the wall!"

Michael Bascom grew strangely pale, yet he affected utter incredulity.

"Poor child," he said kindly; "you have been fretting about your father until your nerves are in a weak state, and you are full of fancies. A shadow in the corner, indeed; why, at daybreak, every corner is full of shadows. My old coat, flung upon a chair, will make you as good a ghost as you need care to see."

"Oh, sir, I have tried to think it is my fancy. But I have had the same burden weighing me down every night. I have seen the same shadow every morning."

"But when broad daylight comes, can you not see what stuff your shadow is made of?"

"No, sir; the shadow goes before it is broad daylight."

"Of course, just like other shadows. Come, come, get these silly notions out of your head, or you will never do for the work-a-day world. I could easily speak to Mrs. Skegg, and make her give you another room, if I wanted to encourage you in your folly. But that would be about the worst thing I could do for you. Besides, she tells me that all the other rooms on that floor are damp; and, no doubt, if she shifted you into one of them, you would discover another shadow in another corner, and get rheumatism into the bargain. No, my good girl, you must try to prove yourself the better for a superior education."

"I will do my best, sir," Maria answered meekly, dropping a curtsey.

Maria went back to the kitchen sorely depressed. It was a dreary life she led at Wildheath Grange—dreary by day, awful by night; for the vague burden and the shapeless shadow, which seemed so slight a matter to the elderly scholar, were unspeakably terrible to her. Nobody had told her that the house was haunted; yet she walked about those echoing passages wrapped round with a cloud of fear. She had no pity from Daniel Skegg and his wife. Those two pious souls had made up their minds that the character of the house should be upheld, so far as Maria went. To her, as a foreigner, the Grange should be maintained to be an immaculate dwelling, tainted by no sulphurous blast from the under world. A willing, biddable girl had become a necessary element in the existence of Mrs. Skegg. That girl had been found and that girl must be kept. Any fancies of a supernatural character must be put down with a high hand.

"Ghosts, indeed!" cried the amiable Skegg. "Read your Bible, Maria, and don't talk no more about ghosts."

"There are ghosts in the Bible," said Maria, with a shiver at the recollection of certain awful passages in the Scripture she knew so well.

"Ah, they was in their right place, or they wouldn't ha' been there," retorted Mrs. Skegg. "You ain't agoin' to pick holes in your Bible, I hope, Mariar, at your time of life."

Maria sat down quietly in her corner by the kitchen fire, and turned over the leaves of her dead father's Bible till she came to the chapters they two had loved best and oftenest read together. He had been a simple-minded, straightforward man, the Yarmouth cabinet-maker—a man full of aspirations after good, innately refined, instinctively religious. He and his motherless girl had spent their lives alone together, in the neat little home, which Maria had so soon learnt to cherish and beautify; and they had loved each other with an almost romantic love. They had had the same tastes, the same ideas. Very little had sufficed to make them happy. But inexorable death parted father and daughter, in one of those sharp sudden partings which are like the shock of an earthquake—instantaneous ruin, desolation and despair.

Maria's fragile form had bent before the tempest. She had lived through a trouble that might have crushed a stronger nature. Her deep religious convictions, and her belief that this cruel parting would not be for ever, had sustained her. She faced life, and its cares and duties, with a gentle patience which was the noblest form of courage.

Michael Bascom told himself that the servant-girl's foolish fancy about the room that had been given her was not a matter for serious consideration. Yet the idea dwelt in his mind unpleasantly, and disturbed him at his labours. The exact sciences require the complete power of a man's brain, his undistracted attention;

and on this particular evening Michael found that he was only giving his work a part of his attention. The girl's pale face, the girl's tremulous tones, thrust themselves into the foreground of his thoughts.

He closed his book with a fretful sigh, wheeled his large arm-chair round to the fire, and gave himself up to contemplation. To attempt study with so disturbed a mind was useless. It was a dull grey evening, early in November; the student's reading-lamp was lighted, but the shutters were not yet shut, nor the curtains drawn. He could see the leaden sky outside his windows, the fir-tree tops tossing in the angry wind. He could hear the wintry blast whistling amidst the gables, before it rushed off seaward with a savage howl that sounded like a war-whoop.

Michael Bascom shivered, and drew nearer the fire.

"It's childish, foolish nonsense," he said to himself, "yet it's strange she should have that fancy about the shadow; for they say Anthony Bascom destroyed himself in that room. I remember hearing it when I was a boy, from an old servant whose mother was housekeeper at the great house in Anthony's time, I never heard how he died, poor fellow—whether he poisoned himself, or shot himself, or cut his throat; but I've been told that was the room. Old Skegg has heard it too. I could see that by his manner when he told me the girl was to sleep there."

He sat for a long time, till the grey of evening outside his study windows changed to the black of night, and the war-whoop of the wind died away to a low complaining murmur. He sat looking into the fire, and letting his thoughts wander back to the past and the traditions he had heard in his boyhood.

That was a sad, foolish story of his great-uncle, Anthony Bascom: the pitiful story of a wasted fortune and a wasted life. A riotous collegiate career at Cambridge, a racing-stable at Newmarket, an imprudent marriage, a dissipated life in London, a runaway wife, an estate forfeited to Jew money-lenders, and then the fatal end.

Michael had often heard that dismal story; how, when Anthony Bascom's fair false wife had left him, when his credit was exhausted, and his friends had grown tired of him, and all was gone except Wildheath Grange, Anthony, the broken-down man of fashion, had come to that lonely house unexpectedly one night, and had ordered his bed to be got ready for him in the room where he used to sleep when he came to the place for the wild duck shooting, in his boyhood. His old blunderbuss was still hanging over the mantelpiece, where he had left it when he came into the property, and could afford to buy the newest thing in fowling-pieces. He had not been to Wildheath for fifteen years; nay, for a good many of those years he had almost forgotten that the dreary old house belonged to him.

The woman who had been housekeeper at Bascom Park, till house and lands had passed into the hands of the Jews, was at this time the sole occupant of Wildheath. She cooked some supper for her master, and made him as comfortable as she could in the long untenanted dining-room; but she was distressed to find, when she cleared the table after he had gone upstairs to bed, that he had eaten hardly anything.

Next morning she got his breakfast ready in the same room, which she managed to make brighter and cheerier than it had looked overnight. Brooms, dusting-brushes, and a good fire did much to improve the aspect of things. But the morning wore on to noon, and the old housekeeper listened in vain for her master's footfall on the stairs. Noon waned to late afternoon. She had made no at-tempt to disturb him, thinking that he had worn himself out by a tedious journey on horseback, and that he was sleeping the sleep of exhaustion. But when the brief November day clouded with the first shadows of twilight, the old woman grew seriously alarmed, and went upstairs to her master's door, where she waited in vain for any reply to her repeated calls and knockings.

The door was locked on the inside, and the housekeeper was not strong enough to break it open. She rushed downstairs again full of fear, and ran bare-headed out into the lonely road. There was no habitation nearer than the turnpike on the old coach road, from which this side road branched off to the sea. There was scanty hope of a chance passer-by. The old woman ran along the road, hardly knowing whither she was going or what she was going to do, but with a vague idea that she must get somebody to help her.

Chance favoured her. A cart, laden with sea-weed, came lumbering slowly along from the level line of sands yonder where the land melted into water. A heavy lumbering farm-labourer walked beside the cart.

"For God's sake, come in and burst open my master's door!" she entreated, seizing the man by the arm. "He's lying dead, or in a fit, and I can't get to help him."

"All right, missus," answered the man, as if such an invitation were a matter of daily occurrence. "Whoa, Dobbin; stond still, horse, and be donged to thee."

Dobbin was glad enough to be brought to anchor on the patch of waste grass in front of the Grange garden. His master followed the housekeeper upstairs, and shattered the old-fashioned box-lock with one blow of his ponderous fist.

The old woman's worst fear was realised. Anthony Bascom was dead. But the mode and manner of his death Michael had never been able to learn. The housekeeper's daughter, who told him the story, was an old woman when he was a boy. She had only shaken her head, and looked unutterable things, when he questioned her too closely. She had never even admitted that the old squire had committed suicide. Yet the tradition of his self-destruction was rooted in the minds of the natives of Holcroft: and there was a settled belief that his ghost, at certain times and seasons, haunted Wildheath Grange.

Now Michael Bascom was a stern materialist. For him the universe, with all its inhabitants, was but a stupendous machine, governed by inexorable laws. To such a man the idea of a ghost was simply absurd—as absurd as the assertion that two and two make five, or that a circle can be formed of a straight line. Yet he had a kind of dilettante interest in the idea of a mind which could believe in ghosts. The subject offered a curious psychological study. This poor little pale girl, now, had evidently got some supernatural terror into her head, which could only be conquered by rational treatment.

"I know what I ought to do," Michael Bascom said to himself suddenly. "I'll occupy that room myself tonight, and demonstrate to this foolish girl that her notion about the shadow is nothing more than a silly fancy, bred of timidity and low spirits. An ounce of proof is better than a pound of argument. If I can prove to her that I have spent a night in the room, and seen no such shadow, she will understand what an idle thing superstition is."

Daniel came in presently to shut the shutters.

"Tell your wife to make up my bed in the room where Maria has been sleeping, and to put her into one of the rooms on the first floor for tonight, Skegg," said Mr. Bascom.

"Sir?"

Mr. Bascom repeated his order.

"That silly wench has been complaining to you about her room," Skegg exclaimed indignantly. "She doesn't deserve to be well fed and cared for in a comfortable home. She ought to go to the workhouse."

"Don't be angry with the poor girl, Skegg. She has taken a foolish fancy into her head, and I want to show her how silly she is," said Mr. Bascom.

"And you want to sleep in his———in that room yourself," said the butler.

"Precisely."

"Well," mused Skegg, "if he does walk—which I don't believe—he was your own flesh and blood; and I don't suppose he'll do you any hurt."

When Daniel Skegg went back to the kitchen he railed mercilessly at poor Maria, who sat pale and silent in her corner by the hearth, darning old Mrs. Skegg's grey worsted stockings, which were the roughest and harshest covering that ever human foot clothed itself withal. "Was there ever such a whimsical, fine, lady-like miss," demanded Daniel, "to come into a gentleman's house, and drive him out of his own bedroom to sleep in an attic, with her nonsenses and vagaries." If this was the result of being educated above one's station, Daniel declared that he was thankful he had never got so far in his schooling as to read words of two syllables without spelling. Education might be hanged, for him, if this was all it led to.

"I am very sorry," faltered Maria, weeping silently over her work. "Indeed, Mr. Skegg, I made no complaint. My master questioned me, and I told him the truth. That was all."

"All!" exclaimed Mr. Skegg irately; "all, indeed! I should think it was enough."

Poor Maria held her peace. Her mind, fluttered by Daniel's unkindness, had wandered away from that bleak big kitchen to the lost home of the past—the snug little parlour where she and her father had sat beside the cosy hearth on such a night as this; she with her smart work-box and her plain sewing, he with the newspaper he loved to read; the petted cat purring on the rug, the kettle singing on the bright brass trivet, the tea tray pleasantly suggestive of the most comfortable meal in the day.

Oh, those happy nights, that dear companionship! Were they really gone for ever, leaving nothing behind them but unkindness and servitude?

Michael Bascom retired later than usual that night. He was in the habit of sitting at his books long after every other lamp but his own had been extinguished. The Skeggs had subsided into silence and darkness in their dreary ground-floor bed-chamber. Tonight his studies were of a peculiarly interesting kind, and belonged to the order of recreative reading rather than of hard work. He was deep in the history of that mysterious people who had their dwelling-place in the Swiss lakes, and was much exercised by certain speculations and theories about them.

The old eight-day clock on the stairs was striking two as Michael slowly ascended, candle in hand, to the hitherto unknown region of the attics. At the top of the staircase he found himself facing a dark narrow passage which led northwards, a passage that was in itself sufficient to strike terror to a superstitious mind, so black and uncanny did it look.

"Poor child," mused Mr. Bascom, thinking of Maria; "this attic floor is rather dreary, and for a young mind prone to fancies———"

He had opened the door of the north room by this time, and stood looking about him.

It was a large room, with a ceiling that sloped on one side, but was fairly lofty upon the other; an old-fashioned room, full of old-fashioned furniture—big, ponderous, clumsy—associated with a day that was gone and people that were dead. A walnut-wood wardrobe stared him in the face—a wardrobe with brass handles, which gleamed out of the darkness like diabolical eyes. There was a tall four-post bedstead, which had been cut down on one side to accommodate the slope of the ceiling, and which had a misshapen and deformed aspect in consequence. There was an old mahogany bureau, that smelt of secrets. There were some heavy old chairs with rush bottoms, mouldy with age, and much worn. There was a corner washstand, with a big basin and a small jug—the odds and ends of past years. Carpet there was none, save a narrow strip beside the bed.

"It is a dismal room," mused Michael, with the same touch of pity for Maria's weakness which he had felt on the landing just now.

To him it mattered nothing where he slept; but having let himself down to a lower level by his interest in the Swiss lake-people, he was in a manner humanised by the lightness of his evening's reading, and was even inclined to compassionate the feebleness of a foolish girl.

He went to bed, determined to sleep his soundest. The bed was comfortable, well supplied with blankets, rather luxurious than otherwise, and the scholar had that agreeable sense of fatigue which promises profound and restful slumber.

He dropped off to sleep quickly, but woke with a start ten minutes afterwards. What was this consciousness of a burden of care that had awakened him—this sense of all-pervading trouble that weighed upon his spirits and oppressed his heart—this icy horror of some terrible crisis in life through which be must inevitably pass? To him these feelings were as novel as they were painful. His life had flowed on with smooth and sluggish tide, unbroken by so much as a ripple of sorrow. Yet tonight he felt all the pangs of unavailing remorse; the agonising memory of a life wasted; the stings of humiliation and disgrace, shame, ruin; the foreshadowing of a hideous death, which he had doomed himself to die by his own hand. These were the horrors that pressed him round and weighed him down as he lay in Anthony Bascom's room.

Yes, even he, the man who could recognise nothing in nature, or in nature's God, better or higher than an irresponsible and invariable machine governed by mechanical laws, was fain to admit that here he found himself face to face with a psychological mystery. This trouble, which came between him and sleep, was the trouble that had pursued Anthony Bascom on the last night of his life. So had the suicide felt as he lay in that lonely room, perhaps striving to rest his wearied brain with one last earthly sleep before he passed to the unknown intermediate land where all is darkness and slumber. And that troubled mind had haunted the room ever since. It was not the ghost of the man's body that returned to the spot where he had suffered and perished, but the ghost of his mind—his very self; no meaningless simulacrum of the clothes he wore, and the figure that filled them.

Michael Bascom was not the man to abandon his high ground of sceptical philosophy without a struggle. He tried his hardest to conquer this oppression that weighed upon mind and sense. Again and again he succeeded in composing himself to sleep, but only to wake again and again to the same torturing thoughts, the same remorse, the same despair. So the night passed in unutterable weariness; for though he told himself that the trouble was not his trouble, that there was no reality in the burden, no reason for the remorse, these vivid fancies were as painful as realities, and took as strong a hold upon him.

The first streak of light crept in at the window—dim, and cold, and grey; then came twilight, and he looked at the corner between the wardrobe and the door.

Yes; there was the shadow: not the shadow of the wardrobe only—that was clear enough, but a vague and shapeless something which darkened the dull brown wall; so faint, so shadowy, that he could form no conjecture as to its nature, or the thing it represented. He determined to watch this shadow till broad daylight; but the weariness of the night had exhausted him, and before the first dimness of dawn had passed away he had fallen fast asleep, and was tasting the blessed balm of undisturbed slumber. When he woke the winter sun was shining in at the lattice, and the room had lost its gloomy aspect. It looked old-fashioned, and grey, and brown, and shabby; but the depth of its gloom had fled with the shadows and the darkness of night.

Mr. Bascom rose refreshed by a sound sleep, which had lasted nearly three hours. He remembered the wretched feelings which had gone before that renovating slumber; but he recalled his strange sensations only to despise them, and he despised himself for having attached any importance to them.

"Indigestion very likely," he told himself; "or perhaps mere fancy, engendered of that foolish girl's story. The wisest of us is more under the dominion of imagination than he would care to confess. Well, Maria shall not sleep in this room any more. There is no particular reason why she should, and she shall not be made unhappy to please old Skegg and his wife.

When he had dressed himself in his usual leisurely way, Mr. Bascom walked up to the corner where he had seen or imagined the shadow, and examined the spot carefully.

At first sight he could discover nothing of a mysterious character. There was no door in the papered wall, no trace of a door that had been there in the past. There was no trap-door in the worm-eaten boards. There was no dark ineradicable stain to hint at murder. There was not the faintest suggestion of a secret or a mystery.

He looked up at the ceiling. That was sound enough, save for a dirty patch here and there where the rain had blistered it.

Yes; there was something—an insignificant thing, yet with a suggestion of grimness which startled him.

About a foot below the ceiling he saw a large iron hook projecting from the wall, just above the spot where he had seen the shadow of a vaguely defined form. He mounted on a chair the better to examine this hook, and to understand, if he could, the purpose for which it had been put there.

It was old and rusty. It must have been there for many years. Who could have placed it there, and why? It was not the kind of hook upon which one would hang a picture or one's garments. It was placed in an obscure corner. Had Anthony Bascom put it there on the night he died; or did he find it there ready for a fatal use?

"If I were a superstitious man," thought Michael; "I should be inclined to believe that Anthony Bascom hung himself from that rusty old hook."

"Sleep well, sir?" asked Daniel, as he waited upon his master at breakfast.

"Admirably," answered Michael, determined not to gratify the man's curiosity.

He had always resented the idea that Wildheath Grange was haunted.

"Oh, indeed, sir. You were so late that I fancied——"

"Late, yes! I slept so well that I overshot my usual hour for waking. But, by-the-way, Skegg, as that poor girl objects to the room, let her sleep somewhere else. It can't make any difference to us, and it may make some difference to her."

"Humph!" muttered Daniel in his grumpy way; you didn't see anything queer up there, did you?"

"See anything? Of course not."

"Well, then, why should she see things? It's all her silly fiddle-faddle."

"Never mind, let her sleep in another room."

"There ain't another room on the top floor that's dry."

"Then let her sleep on the floor below. She creeps about quietly enough, poor little timid thing. She won't disturb me."

Daniel grunted, and his master understood the grunt to mean obedient assent; but here Mr. Bascom was unhappily mistaken. The proverbial obstinacy of the pig family is as nothing compared with the obstinacy of a cross-grained old man, whose narrow mind has never been illuminated by education. Daniel was beginning to feel jealous of his master's compassionate interest in the orphan girl. She was a sort of gentle clinging thing that might creep into an elderly bachelor's heart unawares, and make herself a comfortable nest there.

"We shall have fine carryings-on, and me and my old woman will be no-where, if I don't put down my heel pretty strong upon this nonsense," Daniel muttered to himself, as he carried the breakfast-tray to the pantry.

Maria met him in the passage.

"Well, Mr. Skegg, what did my master say?" she asked breathlessly. "Did he see anything strange in the room?"

"No, girl. What should he see? He said you were a fool."

"Nothing disturbed him? And he slept there peacefully?" faltered Maria.

"Never slept better in his life. Now don't you begin to feel ashamed of yourself?"

"Yes," she answered meekly; "I am ashamed of being so full of fancies. I will go back to my room tonight, Mr. Skegg, if you like and I will never complain of it again."

"I hope you won't," snapped Skegg; "you've given us trouble enough already."

Maria sighed, and went about her work in saddest silence. The day wore slowly on, like all other days in that lifeless old house. The scholar sat in his study;

Maria moved softly from room to room, sweeping and dusting in the cheerless solitude. The mid-day sun faded into the grey of afternoon, and evening came down like a blight upon the dull old house.

Throughout that day Maria and her master never met. Anyone who had been so far interested in the girl as to observe her appearance would have seen that she was unusually pale, and that her eyes had a resolute look, as of one who was resolved to face a painful ordeal. She ate hardly anything all day. She was curiously silent. Skegg and his wife put down both these symptoms to temper.

"She won't eat and she won't talk," said Daniel to the partner of his joys. "That means sulkiness, and I never allowed sulkiness to master me when I was a young man, and you tried it on as a young woman, and I'm not going to be conquered by sulkiness in my old age."

Bed-time came, and Maria bade the Skeggs a civil good-night, and went up to her lonely garret without a murmur.

The next morning came, and Mrs. Skegg looked in vain for her patient handmaiden, when she wanted Maria's services in preparing the breakfast.

"The wench sleeps sound enough this morning," said the old woman. "Go and call her, Daniel. My poor legs can't stand them stairs."

"Your poor legs are getting uncommon useless," muttered Daniel testily, as he went to do his wife's behest.

He knocked at the door, and called Maria—once, twice, thrice, many times; but there was no reply. He tried the door, and found it locked. He shook the door violently, cold with fear.

Then he told himself that the girl had played him a trick. She had stolen away before daybreak, and left the door locked to frighten him. But, no; this could not be, for he could see the key in the lock when he knelt down and put his eye to the keyhole. The key prevented his seeing into the room.

"She's in there, laughing in her sleeve at me," he told himself; "but I'll soon be even with her."

There was a heavy bar on the staircase, which was intended to secure the shutters of the window that lighted the stairs. It was a detached bar, and always stood in a corner near the window, which it was but rarely employed to fasten. Daniel ran down to the landing, and seized upon this massive iron bar, and then ran back to the garret door.

One blow from the heavy bar shattered the old lock, which was the same lock the carter had broken with his strong fist seventy years before. The door flew open, and Daniel went into the attic which he had chosen for the stranger's bed-chamber.

Maria was hanging from the hook in the wall. She had contrived to cover her face decently with her handkerchief. She had hanged herself deliberately about an hour before Daniel found her, in the early grey of morning. The doctor, who was summoned from Holcroft, was able to declare the time at which she had slain herself, but there was no one who could say what sudden access of terror had impelled her to the desperate act, or under what slow torture of nervous apprehension her mind had given way. The coroner's jury returned the customary merciful verdict of "Temporary insanity."

The girl's melancholy fate darkened the rest of Michael Bascom's life. He fled from Wildheath Grange as from an accursed spot, and from the Skeggs as from the murderers of a harmless innocent girl. He ended his days at Oxford, where he found the society of congenial minds, and the books he loved. But the memory of Maria's sad face, and sadder death, was his abiding sorrow. Out of that deep shadow his soul was never lifted.

THE GHOST AT THE RATH[*]

Rosa Mulholland

Many may disbelieve this story, yet there are some still living who can remember hearing, when children, of the events which it details, and of the strange sensation which their publicity excited. The tale, in its present form, is copied, by permission, from a memoir written by the chief actor in the romance, and preserved as a sort of heirloom in the family whom it concerns.

In the year —— I, John Thunder, Captain in the —— Regiment, having passed many years abroad following my profession, received notice that I had become owner of certain properties which I had never thought to inherit. I set off for my native land, arrived in Dublin, found that my good fortune was real, and at once began to look about me for old friends. The first I met with, quite by accident, was curly-headed Frank O'Brien, who had been at school with me, though I was ten years his senior. He was curly-headed still, and handsome, as he had promised to be, but careworn and poor. During an evening spent at his chambers I drew all his history from him. He was a briefless barrister. As a man he was not more talented than he had been as a boy. Hard work and anxiety had not brought him success, only broken his health and soured his mind. He was in love, and he could not marry. I soon knew all about Mary Leonard, his *fiancée*, whom he had met at a house in the country somewhere, in which she was governess. They had now been engaged for two years—she active and hopeful, he sick and despondent. From the letters of hers which he showed me, I thought she was worth all the devotion he felt for her. I considered a good deal about what could be done for Frank, but I could not easily hit upon a plan to assist him. For ten chances you have of helping a sharp man, you have not two for a dull one.

In the meantime my friend must regain his health, and a change of air and scene was necessary. I urged him to make a voyage of discovery to the Rath, an old house

[*] "The Ghost at the Rath" was originally published in *The Irish Monthly* in December 1886 and was later included in Mulholland's collection *The Haunted Organist of Hurly Burly and Other Stories* (London: Hutchinson, [1891]). The current text is based on the 1891 edition. Obvious typographical errors and inconsistencies have been silently corrected.

and park which had come into my possession as portion of my recently acquired estates. I had never been to the place myself; but it had once been the residence of Sir Luke Thunder, of generous memory, and I knew that it was furnished, and provided with a caretaker. I pressed him to leave Dublin at once, and promised to follow him as soon as I found it possible to do so.

So Frank went down to the Rath. The place was two hundred miles away; he was a stranger there, and far from well. When the first week came to an end, and I had heard nothing from him, I did not like the silence; when a fortnight had passed, and still not a word to say he was alive, I felt decidedly uncomfortable; and when the third week of his absence arrived at Saturday without bringing me news, I found myself whizzing through a part of the country I had never travelled before, in the same train in which I had seen Frank seated at our parting.

I reached D ——, and, shouldering my knapsack, walked right into the heart of a lovely wooded country. Following the directions I had received, I made my way to a lonely road, on which I met not a soul, and which seemed cut out of the heart of a forest, so closely were the trees ranked on either side, and so dense was the twilight made by the meeting and intertwining of the thick branches overhead. In these shades I came upon a gate, like a gate run to seed, with tall, thin, brick pillars, brandishing long grasses from their heads, and spotted with a melancholy crust of creeping moss. I jangled a cracked bell, and an old man appeared from the thickets within, stared at me, then admitted me with a rusty key. I breathed freely on hearing that my friend was well and to be seen. I presented a letter to the old man, having a fancy not to avow myself.

I found my friend walking up and down the alleys of a neglected orchard, with the lichened branches tangled above his head, and ripe apples rotting about his feet. His hands were locked behind his back, and his head was set on one side, listening to the singing of a bird. I never had seen him look so well; yet there was a vacancy about his whole air which I did not like. He did not seem at all surprised to see me, asked had he really not written to me; thought he had; was so comfortable that he had forgotten everything else. He fancied he had only been there about three days; could not imagine how the time had passed. He seemed to talk wildly, and this, coupled with the unusual happy placidity of his manner, confounded me. The place knew him, he told me confidentially; the place belonged to him, or should; the birds sang him this, the very trees bent before him as he passed, the air whispered him that he had been long expected, and should be poor no more.

Wrestling with my judgment ere it might pronounce him mad, I followed him indoors. The Rath was no ordinary old country-house. The acres around it were so wildly overgrown that it was hard to decide which had been pleasure-ground and where the thickets had begun. The plan of the house was fine, with mullioned windows, and here and there a fleck of stained glass flinging back the challenge of an angry sunset. The vast rooms were full of a dusky glare from the sky as I strolled through them in the twilight. The antique furniture had many a blood-red stain on the abrupt notches of its dark carvings; the dusty mirrors flared back at the windows, while the faded curtains produced streaks of uncertain colour from the depths of their sullen foldings.

Dinner was laid for us in the library, a long wainscoted room, with an enormous fire roaring up the chimney, sending a dancing light over the dingy titles of long unopened books. The old man who had unlocked the gate for me served us at table, and, after drawing the dusty curtains, and furnishing us with a plentiful supply of fuel and wine, left us. His clanking hobnailed shoes went echoing away in the distance over the unmatted tiles of the vacant hall till a door closed with a resounding clang very far away, letting us know that we were shut up together for the night in this vast, mouldy, oppressive old house.

I felt as if I could scarcely breathe in it. I could not eat with my usual appetite. The air of the place seemed heavy and tainted. I grew sick and restless. The very wine tasted badly, as if it had been drugged. I had a strange feeling that I had been in the house before, and that something evil had happened to me in it. Yet such could not be the case. What puzzled me most was, that I should feel dissatisfied at seeing Frank looking so well, and eating so heartily. A little time before I should have been glad to suffer something to see him as he looked now; and yet not quite as he looked now. There was a drowsy contentment about him which I could not understand. He did not talk of his work, or of any wish to return to it. He seemed to have no thought of anything but the delight of hanging about that old house, which had certainly cast a spell over him.

About midnight he seized a light, and proposed retiring to our rooms. "I have such delightful dreams in this place," he said. He volunteered, as we issued into the hall, to take me upstairs and show me the upper regions of his paradise. I said, "Not to-night." I felt a strange creeping sensation as I looked up the vast black staircase, wide enough for a coach to drive down, and at the heavy darkness bending over it like a curse, while our lamps made drips of light down the first two or three gloomy steps. Our bedrooms were on the ground floor, and stood opposite one another off a passage which led to a garden. Into mine Frank conducted me, and left me for his own.

The uneasy feeling which I have described did not go from me with him, and I felt a restlessness amounting to pain when left alone in my chamber. Efforts had evidently been made to render the room habitable, but there was a something antagonistic to sleep in every angle of its many crooked corners. I kicked chairs out of their prim order along the wall, and banged things about here and there; finally, thinking that a good night's rest was the best cure for an inexplicably disturbed frame of mind, I undressed as quickly as possible, and laid my head on my pillow under a canopy, like the wings of a gigantic bird of prey wheeling above me ready to pounce.

But I could not sleep. The wind grumbled in the chimney, and the boughs swished in the garden outside; and between these noises I thought I heard sounds coming from the interior of the old house, where all should have been still as the dead down in their vaults. I could not make out what these sounds were. Sometimes I thought I heard feet running about, sometimes I could have sworn there were double knocks, tremendous tantarararas at the great hall door. Sometimes I heard the clashing of dishes, the echo of voices calling, and the dragging about of furniture. Whilst I sat up in bed trying to account for these noises, my door suddenly flew open, a bright light streamed in from the passage without, and a powdered servant in an elaborate livery of antique pattern stood holding the handle of the door in his hand, and bowing low to me in the bed.

"Her ladyship, my mistress, desires your presence in the drawing-room, sir."

This was announced in the measured tone of a well-trained domestic. Then with another bow he retired, the door closed, and I was left in the dark to determine whether I had not suddenly awakened from a tantalising dream. In spite of my very wakeful sensations, I believe I should have endeavoured to convince myself that I had been sleeping, but that I perceived light shining under my door, and through the keyhole, from the passage. I got up, lit my lamp, and dressed myself as hastily as I was able.

I opened my door, and the passage down which a short time before I had almost groped my way, with my lamp blinking in the dense foggy darkness, was now illuminated with a light as bright as gas. I walked along it quickly, looking right and left to see whence the glare proceeded. Arriving at the hall, I found it also blazing with light, and filled with perfume. Groups of choice plants, heavy with blossoms, made it look like a garden. The mosaic floor was strewn with costly mats. Soft colours and gilding shone from the walls, and canvases that had been black gave forth faces of men and women looking brightly from their burnished frames. Servants were running about, the dining-room and drawing-room doors were opening and shutting, and as I looked through each I saw vistas of light and colour, the moving of brilliant crowds, the waving of feathers, and glancing of brilliant dresses and uniforms. A festive hum reached me with a drowsy subdued sound, as if I were listening with stuffed ears. Standing aside by an orange tree, I gave up speculating on what this might be, and concentrated all my powers on observation.

Wheels were heard suddenly, and a resounding knock banged at the door till it seemed that the very rooks in the chimneys must be startled screaming out of their nests. The door flew open, a flaming of lanterns was seen outside, and a dazzling lady came up the steps and swept into the hall. When she held up her cloth of silver train, I could see the diamonds that twinkled on her feet. Her bosom was covered with roses, and there was a red light in her eyes like the reflection from a hundred glowing fires. Her black hair went coiling about her head, and couched among the braids lay a jewel not unlike the head of a snake. She was flashing and glowing with gems and flowers. Her beauty and brilliance made me dizzy. There came a faintness in the air, as if her breath had poisoned it. A whirl of storm came in with her, and rushed up the staircase like a moan. The plants shuddered and shed their blossoms, and all the lights grew dim a moment, then flared up again.

Now the drawing-room door opened, and a gentleman came out with a young girl leaning on his arm. He was a fine-looking, middle-aged gentleman, with a mild countenance.

The girl was a slender creature, with golden hair and a pale face. She was dressed in pure white, with a large ruby like a drop of blood at her throat. They advanced together to receive the lady who had arrived. The gentleman offered his arm to the stranger, and the girl who was displaced for her fell back, and walked behind them with a downcast air. I felt irresistibly impelled to follow them, and passed with them into the drawing-room. Never had I mixed in a finer, gayer crowd. The costumes were rich and of an old-fashioned pattern. Dancing was going forward with spirit—minuets and country dances. The stately gentleman was evidently the host, and moved among the company, introducing the magnificent lady right and left. He led her to the head of the room presently, and they mixed in the dance. The arrogance of her manner and the fascination of her beauty were wonderful.

I cannot attempt to describe the strange manner in which I was in this company, and yet not of it. I seemed to view all I beheld through some fine and subtle medium. I saw clearly, yet I felt that it was not with my ordinary naked eyesight. I can compare it to nothing but looking at a scene through a piece of smoked or coloured glass. And just in the same way (as I have said before) all sounds seemed to reach me as if I were listening with ears imperfectly stuffed. No one present took any notice of me. I spoke to several, and they made no reply—did not even turn their eyes upon me, nor show in any way that they heard me. I planted myself straight in the way of a fine fellow in a general's uniform, but he, swerving neither to right nor left by an inch, kept on his way, as though I were a streak of mist, and left me behind him. Every one I touched eluded me somehow. Substantial as they all looked, I could not contrive to lay my hand on anything that felt like solid flesh. Two or three times I felt a momentary relief from the oppressive sensations which distracted me, when I firmly believed I saw Frank's head at some distance among the crowd, now in one room and now in another, and again in the conservatory, which was hung with lamps, and filled with people walking about among the flowers. But, whenever I approached, he had vanished. At last I came upon him, sitting by himself on a couch behind a curtain watching the dancers. I laid my hand upon his shoulder. Here was something substantial at last. He did not look up; he seemed aware neither of my touch nor my speech. I looked in his staring eyes, and found that he was sound asleep. I could not wake him.

Curiosity would not let me remain by his side. I again mixed with the crowd, and found the stately host still leading about the magnificent lady. No one seemed to notice that the golden-haired girl was sitting weeping in a corner; no one but the beauty in the silver train, who sometimes glanced at her contemptuously. Whilst I watched her distress a group came between me and her, and I wandered into another room, where, as though I had turned from one picture of her to look at another, I beheld her dancing gaily, in the full glee of Sir Roger de Coverley, with a fine-looking youth, who was more plainly dressed than any other person in the room. Never was a better-matched pair to look at. Down the middle they danced, hand in hand, his face full of tenderness, hers beaming with joy, right and left bowing and curtseying, parted and meeting again, smiling and whispering;

but over the heads of smaller women there were the fierce eyes of the magnificent beauty scowling at them. Then again the crowd shifted around me, and this scene was lost.

For some time I could see no trace of the golden-haired girl in any of the rooms. I looked for her in vain, till at last I caught a glimpse of her standing smiling in a doorway with her finger lifted, beckoning. At whom? Could it be at me? Her eyes were fixed on mine. I hastened into the hall, and caught sight of her white dress passing up the wide black staircase from which I had shrunk some hours earlier. I followed her, she keeping some steps in advance. It was intensely dark, but by the gleaming of her gown I was able to trace her flying figure. Where we went, I knew not, up how many stairs, down how many passages, till we arrived at a low-roofed large room with sloping roof and queer windows where there was a dim light, like the sanctuary light in a deserted church. Here, when I entered, the golden head was glimmering over something which I presently discerned to be a cradle wrapped round with white curtains, and with a few fresh flowers fastened up on the hood of it, as if to catch a baby's eye. The fair sweet face looked up at me with a glow of pride on it, smiling with happy dimples. The white hands unfolded the curtains, and stripped back the coverlet. Then, suddenly there went a rushing moan all round the weird room, that seemed like a gust of wind forcing in through the crannies, and shaking the jingling old windows in their sockets. The cradle was an empty one. The girl fell back with a look of horror on her pale face that I shall never forget, then, flinging her arms above her head, she dashed from the room.

I followed her as fast as I was able, but the wild white figure was too swift for me. I had lost her before I reached the bottom of the staircase. I searched for her, first in one room, then in another, neither could I see her foe (as I already believed to be), the lady of the silver train. At length I found myself in a small ante-room, where a lamp was expiring on the table. A window was open, close by it the golden-haired girl was lying sobbing in a chair, while the magnificent lady was bending over her as if soothingly, and offering her something to drink in a goblet. The moon was rising behind the two figures. The shuddering light of the lamp was flickering over the girl's bright head, the rich embossing of the golden cup, the lady's silver robes, and, I thought, the jewelled eyes of the serpent looked out from her bending head.

As I watched, the girl raised her face and drank, then suddenly dashed the goblet away; while a cry such as I never heard but once, and shiver to remember, rose to the very roof of the old house, and the clear sharp word *"Poisoned!"* rang and reverberated from hall and chamber in a thousand echoes, like the clash of a peal of bells. The girl dashed herself from the open window, leaving the cry clamouring behind her. I heard the violent opening of doors and running of feet, but I waited for nothing more. Maddened by what I had witnessed, I would have felled the murderess, but she glided unhurt from under my vain blow. I sprang from the window after the wretched white figure. I saw it flying on before me with a speed I could not overtake. I ran till I was dizzy. I called like a madman, and heard the owls croaking back to me. The moon grew huge and bright, the trees grew out before it like the bushy heads of giants, the river lay keen and shining like a long unsheathed sword, couching for deadly work among the rushes. The white figure shimmered and vanished, glittered brightly on before me, shimmered and vanished again, shimmered, staggered, fell, and disappeared in the river. Of what she was, phantom or reality, I thought not at the moment; she had the semblance of a human being going to destruction, and I had the frenzied impulse to save her. I rushed forward with one last effort, struck my foot against the root of a tree, and was dashed to the ground. I remember a crash, momentary pain and confusion; then nothing more.

When my senses returned, the red clouds of the dawn were shining in the river beside me. I arose to my feet, and found that, though much bruised, I was otherwise unhurt. I busied my mind in recalling the strange circumstances which had brought me to that place in the dead of the night. The recollection of all I had witnessed was vividly present to my mind. I took my way slowly to the house, almost expecting to see the marks of wheels and other indications of last night's revel, but the rank grass that covered the gravel was uncrushed, not a blade disturbed, not a stone displaced. I shook one of the drawing-room windows till I shook off the old rusty hasp inside, flung up the creaking sash, and entered. Where were the brilliant draperies and carpets, the soft gilding, the vases teeming with flowers, the thousand sweet odours of the night before? Not a trace of them; no, nor even a ragged cobweb swept away, nor a stiff chair moved an inch from its melancholy place, nor the face of a mirror relieved from one speck of its obscuring dust!

Coming back into the open air, I met the old man from the gate walking up one of the weedy paths. He eyed me meaningly from head to foot, but I gave him good-morrow cheerfully.

"You see I am poking about early," I said.

"I' faith, sir," said he, "an' ye look like a man that had been pokin' about *all night*."

"How so?" said I.

"Why, ye see, sir," said he, "I'm used to 't, an' I can read it in yer face like prent. Some sees one thing an' some another, an' some only feels an' hears. The poor jintleman inside, he says nothin', but he has beautyful dhrames. An' for the Lord's sake, sir, take him out o' this, for I've seen him wandherin' about like a ghost himself in the heart of the night, an' him that sound sleepin' that I couldn't wake him!"

At breakfast I said nothing to Frank of my strange adventures. He had rested well, he said, and boasted of his enchanting dreams. I asked him to describe them, when he grew perplexed and annoyed. He remembered nothing, but that his spirit had been delightfully entertained whilst his body reposed. I now felt a curiosity to go through the old house, and was not surprised, on pushing open a door at the end of a remote mouldy passage, to enter the identical chamber into which I had followed the pale-faced girl when she beckoned me out of the drawing-room. There were the low brooding roof and slanting walls, the short wide latticed windows to which the noonday sun was trying to pierce through a forest of leaves. The hangings rotting with age shook like dreary banners at the opening of the door, and there in the middle of the room was the cradle; only the curtains that had been white were blackened with dirt, and laced and overlaced with cobwebs. I parted the curtains, bringing down a shower of dust upon the floor, and saw lying upon the pillow, within, a child's tiny shoe, and a toy. I need not describe the rest of the house. It was vast and rambling, and, as far as furniture and decorations were concerned, the wreck of grandeur.

Having strange subject for meditation, I walked alone in the orchard that evening. This orchard sloped towards the river I have mentioned before. The trees were old and stunted, and the branches tangled overhead. The ripe apples were rotting in the long bleached grass. A row of taller trees, sycamores and chestnuts, straggled along by the river's edge, ferns and tall weeds grew round and amongst them, and between their trunks, and behind the rifts in the foliage, the water was seen to flow. Walking up and down one of the paths I alternately faced these trees and turned my back upon them. Once when coming towards them I chanced to lift my glance, started, drew my hands across my eyes, looked again, and finally stood still gazing in much astonishment. I saw distinctly the figure of a lady standing by one of the trees, bending low towards the grass. Her face was a little turned away, her dress a bluish-white, her mantle a dun-brown colour. She held a spade in her hand, and her foot was upon it, as if she was in the act of digging. I gazed at her for some time, vainly trying to guess at whom she might be, then I advanced towards her. As I approached, the outlines of her figure broke up and disappeared, and I found that she was only an illusion presented to me by the curious accidental grouping of the lines of two trees which had shaped the space between them into the semblance of the form I have described. A patch of the flowing water had been her robe, a piece of russet moorland her cloak. The spade was an awkward young shoot slanting up from the root of one of the trees. I stepped back and tried to piece her out again bit by bit, but could not succeed.

That night I did not feel at all inclined to return to my dismal chamber, and lie awaiting such another summons as I had once received. When Frank bade me good-night, I heaped fresh coals on the fire, took down from the shelves a book, from which I lifted the dust in layers with my penknife, and, dragging an armchair close to the hearth, tried to make myself as comfortable as might be. I am a strong, robust man, very unimaginative, and little troubled with affections of the nerves, but I confess that my feelings were not enviable, sitting thus alone in that queer old house, with last night's strange pantomime still vividly present to my memory. In spite of my efforts at coolness, I was excited by the prospect of what yet might be in store for me before morning. But these feelings passed away as the night wore on, and I nodded asleep over my book.

I was startled by the sound of a brisk light step walking overhead. Wide awake at once, I sat up and listened. The ceiling was low, but I could not call to mind what room it was that lay above the library in which I sat. Presently I heard the same step upon the stairs, and the loud sharp rustling of a silk dress sweeping against the banisters. The step paused at the library door, and then there was silence. I got up, and with all the courage I could summon seized a light, and opened the door; but there was nothing in the hall but the usual heavy darkness and damp mouldy air. I confess I felt more uncomfortable at that moment than I had done at any time during the preceding night. All the visions that had then appeared to me had produced nothing like the horror of thus feeling a supernatural presence which my eyes were not permitted to behold.

I returned to the library, and passed the night there. Next day I sought for the room above it in which I had heard the footsteps, but could discover no entrance to any such room. Its windows, indeed, I counted from the outside, though they were so overgrown with ivy I could hardly discern them, but in the interior of the house I could find no door to the chamber. I asked Frank about it, but he knew and cared nothing on the subject; I asked the old man at the lodge, and he shook his head.

"Och!" he said, "don't ask about that room. The door's built up, and flesh and blood have no consarn wid it. It was *her own* room."

"Whose own?" I asked.

"Ould Lady Thunder's. An' whist, sir! *that's her grave!*"

"What do you mean?" I said. "Are you out of your mind?"

He laughed queerly, drew nearer, and lowered his voice. "Nobody has asked about the room these years but yourself," he said. "Nobody misses it goin' over the house. My grandfather was an old retainer o' the Thunder family, my father was in the service too, an' I was born myself before the ould lady died. Yon was her room, an' she left her eternal curse on her family if so be they didn't lave her coffin there. *She* wasn't goin' undher the ground to the worms. So there it was left, an' they built up the door. God love ye, sir, an' don't go near it. I wouldn't have told you, only I know ye've seen plenty about already, an' ye have the look o' one that'd be ferretin' things out, savin' yer presence."

He looked at me knowingly, but I gave him no information, only thanked him for putting me on my guard. I could scarcely credit what he told me about the room; but my curiosity was excited regarding it. I made up my mind that day to try and induce Frank to quit the place on the morrow. I felt more and more convinced that the atmosphere was not healthful for his mind, whatever it might be for his body. The sooner we left the spot the better for us both; but the remaining night which I had to pass there I resolved on devoting to the exploring of the walled-up chamber. What impelled me to this resolve I do not know. The undertaking was not a pleasant one, and I should hardly have ventured on it had I been forced to remain much longer at the Rath. But I knew there was little chance of sleep for me in that house, and I thought I might as well go and seek for my adventures as sit waiting for them to come for me, as I had done the night before.

I felt a relish for my enterprise, and expected the night with satisfaction. I did not
say anything of my intention either to Frank or the old man at the lodge. I did not
want to make a fuss, and have my doings talked of all over the country. I may as
well mention here that again, on this evening, when walking in the orchard, I saw
the figure of the lady digging between the trees. And again I saw that this figure
was an illusive appearance; that the water was her gown, and the moorland her
cloak, and a willow in the distance her tresses.

As soon as the night was pretty far advanced, I placed a ladder against the
window which was least covered over with the ivy, and mounted it, having provided myself with a dark lantern. The moon rose full behind some trees that stood
like a black bank against the horizon, and glimmered on the panes as I ripped
away branches and leaves with a knife, and shook the old crazy casement open.
The sashes were rotten, and the fastenings easily gave way. I placed my lantern on
a bench within, and was soon standing beside it in the chamber. The air was insuf-
ferably close and mouldy, and I flung the window open to the widest, and beat
the bowering ivy still further back from about it, so as to let the fresh air of heaven
blow into the place. I then took my lantern in hand, and began to look about me.

The room was vast and double; a velvet curtain hung between me and an
inner chamber. The darkness was thick and irksome, and the scanty light of my
lantern only tantalised me. My eye fell on some tall spectral-looking candelabra
furnished with wax candles, which, though black with age, still bore the marks
of having been guttered by a draught that had blown on them fifty years ago. I
lighted these; they burned up with a ghastly flickering, and the apartment, with
its fittings, was revealed to me. These latter had been splendid in the days of their
freshness: the appointments of the rest of the house were mean in comparison.
The ceiling was painted with fine allegorical figures, also spaces of the walls between the dim mirrors and the sumptuous hangings of crimson velvet, with their
tarnished golden tassels and fringes. The carpet still felt luxurious to the tread, and
the dust could not altogether obliterate the elaborate fancy of its flowery design.
There were gorgeous cabinets laden with curiosities, wonderfully carved chairs,
rare vases, and antique glasses of every description, under some of which lay little
heaps of dust which had once no doubt been blooming flowers. There was a table
laden with books of poetry and science, drawings and drawing materials, which
showed that the occupant of the room had been a person of mind. There was also
a writing-table scattered over with yellow papers, and a work-table at a window,

on which lay reels, a thimble, and a piece of what had once been white muslin, but was now saffron colour, sewn with gold thread, a rusty needle sticking in it. This and the pen lying on the inkstand, the paper-knife between the leaves of a book, the loose sketches shaken out by the side of a portfolio, and the ashes of a fire on the wide mildewed hearth-place, all suggested that the owner of this retreat had been snatched from it without warning, and that whoever had thought proper to build up the doors, had also thought proper to touch nothing that had belonged to her.

Having surveyed all these things, I entered the inner room, which was a bedroom. The furniture of this was in keeping with that of the other chamber. I saw dimly a bed enveloped in lace, and a dressing-table fancifully garnished and draped. Here I espied more candelabra, and going forward to set the lights burning, I stumbled against something. I turned the blaze of my lantern on this something, and started with a sudden thrill of horror. It was a large stone coffin.

I own that I felt very strangely for the next few minutes. When I had recovered the shock, I set the wax-candles burning, and took a better survey of this odd burial-place. A wardrobe stood open, and I saw dresses hanging within. A gown lay upon a chair, as if just thrown off, and a pair of dainty slippers were beside it. The toilet-table looked as if only used yesterday, judging by the litter that covered it; hair-brushes lying this way and that way, essence-bottles with the stoppers out, paint pots uncovered, a ring here, a wreath of artificial flowers there, and in front of all that coffin, the tarnished Cupids that bore the mirror between their hands smirking down at it with a grim complacency.

On the corner of this table was a small golden salver, holding a plate of some black mouldered food, an antique decanter filled with wine, a glass, and a phial with some thick black liquid, uncorked. I felt weak and sick with the atmosphere of the place, and I seized the decanter, wiped the dust from it with my handkerchief, tasted, found that the wine was good, and drank a moderate draught. Immediately it was swallowed I felt a horrid giddiness, and sank upon the coffin. A raging pain was in my head and a sense of suffocation in my chest. After a few intolerable moments I felt better, but the heavy air pressed on me stiflingly, and I rushed from this inner room into the larger and outer chamber. Here a blast of cool air revived me, and I saw that the place was changed.

A dozen other candelabra besides those I had lighted were flaming round the walls, the hearth was all ruddy with a blazing fire, everything that had been dim was bright, the lustre had returned to the gilding, the flowers bloomed in the vases. A lady was sitting before the hearth in a low arm-chair. Her light loose gown swept about her on the carpet, her black hair fell round her to her knees, and into it her hands were thrust as she leaned her forehead upon them, and stared between them into the fire. I had scarcely time to observe her attitude when she turned her head quickly towards me, and I recognised the handsome face of the magnificent lady who had played such a sinister part in the strange scenes that had been enacted before me two nights ago. I saw something dark looming behind her chair, but I thought it was only her shadow thrown backward by the firelight.

She arose and came to meet me, and I recoiled from her. There was something horridly fixed and hollow in her gaze, and filmy in the stirring of her garments. The shadow, as she moved, grew more firm and distinct in outline, and followed her like a servant where she went.

She crossed half of the room, then beckoned me, and sat down at the writing-table. The shadow waited beside her, adjusted her paper, placed the ink-bottle near her and the pen between her fingers. I felt impelled to approach her, and to take my place at her left shoulder, so as to be able to see what she might write. The shadow stood motionless at her other hand. As I became accustomed to the shadow's presence he grew more visibly loathsome and hideous. He was quite distinct from the lady, and moved independently of her with long ugly limbs. She hesitated about beginning to write, and he made a wild gesture with his arm, which brought her hand quickly on the paper, and her pen began to move at once. I needed not to bend and scrutinise in order to read. Every word as it was formed flashed before me like a meteor.

"I am the spirit of Madeline, Lady Thunder, who lived and died in this house, and whose coffin stands in yonder room among the vanities in which I delighted. I am constrained to make my confession to you, John Thunder, who are the present owner of the estates of your family."

Here the hand trembled and stopped writing. But the shadow made a threatening gesture, and the hand fluttered on.

"I was beautiful, poor, and ambitious, and when I entered this house first on the night of a ball given by Sir Luke Thunder, I determined to become its mistress. His daughter, Mary Thunder, was the only obstacle in my way. She divined my intention, and stood between me and her father. She was a gentle, delicate girl, and no match for me. I pushed her aside, and became Lady Thunder. After that I hated her, and made her dread me. I had gained the object of my ambition, but I was jealous of the influence possessed by her over her father, and I revenged myself by crushing the joy out of her young life. In this I defeated my own purpose. She eloped with a young man who was devoted to her, though poor, and beneath her in station. Her father was indignant at first, and my malice was satisfied; but as time passed on I had no children, and she had a son, soon after whose birth her husband died. Then her father took her back to his heart, and the boy was his idol and heir."

Again the hand stopped writing, the ghostly head drooped, and the whole figure was convulsed. But the shadow gesticulated fiercely, and, cowering under its menace, the wretched spirit went on:

"I caused the child to be stolen away. I thought I had done it cunningly, but she tracked the crime home to me. She came and accused me of it, and in the desperation of my terror at discovery, I gave her poison to drink. She rushed from me and from the house in frenzy, and in her mortal anguish fell in the river. People thought she had gone mad from grief for her child, and committed suicide. I only knew the horrible truth. Sorrow brought an illness upon her father, of which he died. Up to the day of his death he had search made for the child. Believing that it was alive, and must be found, he willed all his property to it, his rightful heir, and to its heirs for ever. I buried the deeds under a tree in the orchard, and forged a will, in which all was bequeathed to me during my lifetime. I enjoyed my state and grandeur till the day of my death, which came upon me miserably, and, after that, my husband's possessions went to a distant relation of his family. Nothing more was heard of the fate of the child who was stolen; but he lived and married, and his daughter now toils for her bread—his daughter, who is the rightful owner of all that is said to belong to you, John Thunder. I tell you this that you may devote yourself to the task of discovering this wronged girl, and giving up to her that which you are unlawfully possessed of. Under the thirteenth tree standing on the brink of the river at the foot of the orchard you will find buried the genuine will of Sir Luke Thunder. When you have found and read it, do justice, as you value your soul. In order that you may know the grandchild of Mary Thunder when you find her, you shall behold her in a vision————"

The last words grew dim before me; the lights faded away, and all the place was in darkness, except one spot on the opposite wall. On this spot the light glimmered softly, and against the brightness the outlines of a figure appeared, faintly at first, but, growing firm and distinct, became filled in and rounded at last to the perfect semblance of life. The figure was that of a young girl in a plain black dress, with a bright, happy face, and pale gold hair softly banded on her fair forehead. She might have been the twin-sister of the pale-faced girl whom I had seen bending over the cradle two nights ago; but her healthier, gladder, and prettier sister. When I had gazed on her some moments, the vision faded away as it had come; the last vestige of the brightness died out upon the wall, and I found myself once more in total darkness. Stunned for a time by the sudden changes, I stood watching for the return of the lights and figures; but in vain. By-and-by my eyes grew accustomed to the obscurity, and I saw the sky glimmering behind the little window which I had left open. I could soon discern the writing-table beside me, and possessed myself of the slips of loose paper which lay upon it. I then made my way to the window. The first streaks of dawn were in the sky as I descended my ladder, and I thanked God that I breathed the fresh morning air once more, and heard the cheering sound of the cocks crowing.

All thought of acting immediately upon last night's strange revelations, almost all memory of them, was for the time banished from my mind by the unexpected trouble of the next few days. That morning I found an alarming change in Frank. Feeling sure that he was going to be ill, I engaged a lodging in a cottage in the neighbourhood, whither we removed before nightfall, leaving the accursed Rath behind us. Before midnight he was in the delirium of a raging fever.

I thought it right to let his poor little *fiancée* know his state, and wrote to her, trying to alarm her no more than was necessary. On the evening of the third day after my letter went I was sitting by Frank's bedside, when an unusual bustle outside aroused my curiosity, and going into the cottage kitchen I saw a figure standing in the firelight which seemed a third appearance of that vision of the pale-faced golden-haired girl which was now thoroughly imprinted on my memory,—a third, with all the woe of the first and all the beauty of the second. But this was a living, breathing apparition. She was throwing off her bonnet and shawl, and stood there at home in a moment in her plain black dress. I drew my hand across my eyes to make sure that they did not deceive me. I had beheld so many supernatural visions lately that it seemed as though I could scarcely believe in the reality of anything till I had touched it.

"Oh, sir," said the visitor, "I am Mary Leonard, and are you poor Frank's friend? Oh, sir, we are all the world to one another, and I could not let him die without coming to see him!"

And here the poor little traveller burst into tears. I cheered her as well as I could, telling her that Frank would soon, I trusted, be out of all danger. She told me that she had thrown up her situation in order to come and nurse him. I said we had got a more experienced nurse than she could be, and then I gave her to the care of our landlady, a motherly country-woman. After that I went back to Frank's bedside, nor left it for long till he was convalescent. The fever had swept away all that strangeness in his manner which had afflicted me, and he was quite himself again.

There was a joyful meeting of the lovers. The more I saw of Mary Leonard's bright face the more thoroughly was I convinced that she was the living counterpart of the vision I had seen in the burial chamber. I made inquiries as to her birth, and her father's history, and found that she was indeed the grandchild of that Mary Thunder whose history had been so strangely related to me, and the rightful heiress of all those properties which for a few months only had been mine. Under the tree in the orchard, the thirteenth, and that by which I had seen the lady digging, were found the buried deeds which had been described to me. I made an immediate transfer of property, whereupon some others who thought they had a chance of being my heirs disputed the matter with me, and went to law. Thus the affair has gained publicity, and become a nine days' wonder. Many things have been in my favour, however: the proving of Mary's birth and of Sir Luke's will, the identification of Lady Thunder's handwriting on the slips of paper which I had brought from the burial chamber; also other matters which a search in that chamber brought to light. I triumphed, and I now go abroad, leaving Frank and his Mary made happy by the possession of what could only have been a burden to me.

So the MS. ends. Major Thunder fell in battle a few years after the adventure it relates. Frank O'Brien's grandchildren hear of him with gratitude and awe. The Rath has been long since totally dismantled and left to go to ruin.

FROM THE DEAD[*]

Edith Nesbit

I.

"But true or not true, your brother is a scoundrel. No man—no decent man—tells such things."

"He did not tell me. How dare you suppose it? I found the letter in his desk; and she being my friend and you being her lover, I never thought there could be any harm in my reading her letter to my brother. Give me back the letter. I was a fool to tell you."

Ida Helmont held out her hand for the letter.

"Not yet," I said, and I went to the window. The dull red of a London sunset burned on the paper, as I read in the quaint, dainty handwriting I knew so well and had kissed so often—

"Dear, I do—I do love you; but it's impossible. I must marry Arthur. My honour is engaged. If he would only set me free—but he never will. He loves me so foolishly. But as for me, it is you I love—body, soul, and spirit. There is no one in my heart but you. I think of you all day, and dream of you all night. And we must part. And that is the way of the world. Good-bye!—Yours, yours, yours, Elvire."

I had seen the handwriting, indeed, often enough. But the passion written there was new to me. That I had not seen.

I turned from the window wearily. My sitting-room looked strange to me. There were my books, my reading-lamp, my untasted dinner still on the table, as I had left it when I rose to dissemble my surprise at Ida Helmont's visit—Ida Helmont, who now sat in my easy-chair looking at me quietly.

"Well—do you give me no thanks?"

"You put a knife in my heart, and then ask for thanks?"

"Pardon me," she said, throwing up her chin. "I have done nothing but show

---

[*] "From the Dead" appeared in Nesbit's collection *Grim Tales* (London: Innes, 1893). The current text is based on this edition. Obvious typographical errors and inconsistencies have been silently corrected.

you the truth. For that one should expect no gratitude—may I ask, out of mere curiosity, what you intend to do?"

"Your brother will tell you——"

She rose suddenly, pale to the lips.

"You will not tell my brother?" she began.

"That you have read his private letters? Certainly not!"

She came towards me—her gold hair flaming in the sunset light.

"Why are you so angry with me?" she said. "Be reasonable. What else could I do?"

"I don't know."

"Would it have been right not to tell you?"

"I don't know. I only know that you've put the sun out, and I haven't got used to the dark yet."

"Believe me," she said, coming still nearer to me, and laying her hands in the lightest light touch on my shoulders, "believe me, she never loved you."

There was a softness in her tone that irritated and stimulated me. I moved gently back, and her hands fell by her sides.

"I beg your pardon," I said. "I have behaved very badly. You were quite right to come, and I am not ungrateful. Will you post a letter for me?"

I sat down and wrote—

"I give you back your freedom. The only gift of mine that can please you now. Arthur."

I held the sheet out to Miss Helmont, and, when she had glanced at it, I sealed, stamped, and addressed it.

"Good-bye," I said then, and gave her the letter. As the door closed behind her I sank into my chair, and I am not ashamed to say that I cried like a child or a fool over my lost plaything—the little dark-haired woman who loved someone else with "body, soul, and spirit."

I did not hear the door open or any foot on the floor, and therefore I started when a voice behind me said—

"Are you so very unhappy? Oh, Arthur, don't think I am not sorry for you!"

"I don't want any one to be sorry for me, Miss Helmont," I said.

She was silent a moment. Then, with a quick, sudden, gentle movement she leaned down and kissed my forehead—and I heard the door softly close. Then I knew that the beautiful Miss Helmont loved me.

At first that thought only fleeted by—a light cloud against a grey sky—but the next day reason woke, and said—

"Was Miss Helmont speaking the truth? Was it possible that———?"

I determined to see Elvire, to know from her own lips whether by happy fortune this blow came, not from her, but from a woman in whom love might have killed honesty.

I walked from Hampstead to Gower Street. As I trod its long length, I saw a figure in pink come out of one of the houses. It was Elvire. She walked in front of me to the corner of Store Street. There she met Oscar Helmont. They turned and met me face to face, and I saw all I needed to see. They loved each other. Ida Helmont had spoken the truth. I bowed and passed on. Before six months were gone they were married, and before a year was over I had married Ida Helmont.

What did it I don't know. Whether it was remorse for having, even for half a day, dreamed that she could be so base as to forge a lie to gain a lover, or whether it was her beauty, or the sweet flattery of the preference of a woman who had half her acquaintances at her feet, I don't know; anyhow, my thoughts turned to her as to their natural home. My heart, too, took that road, and before very long I loved her as I had never loved Elvire. Let no one doubt that I loved her—as I shall never love again, please God!

There never was any one like her. She was brave and beautiful, witty and wise, and beyond all measure adorable. She was the only woman in the world. There was a frankness—a largeness of heart—about her that made all other women seem small and contemptible. She loved me and I worshipped her. I married her, I stayed with her for three golden weeks, and then I left her. Why?

Because she told me the truth. It was one night—late—we had sat all the evening in the verandah of our seaside lodging watching the moonlight on the water and listening to the soft sound of the sea on the sand. I have never been so happy; I never shall be happy any more, I hope.

"Heart's heart," she said, leaning her gold head against my shoulder, "how much do you love me?"

"How much?"

"Yes—how much? I want to know what place it is I hold in your heart. Am I more to you than any one else?"

"My love!"

"More than yourself?"

"More than my life!"

"I believe you," she said. Then she drew a long breath, and took my hands in hers. "It can make no difference. Nothing in heaven or earth can come between us now."

"Nothing," I said. "But, sweet, my wife, what is it?"

For she was deathly pale.

"I must tell you," she said; "I cannot hide anything now from you, because I am yours—body, soul, and spirit."

The phrase was an echo that stung me.

The moonlight shone on her gold hair, her warm, soft, gold hair, and on her pale face.

"Arthur," she said, "you remember my coming to you at Hampstead with that letter?"

"Yes, my sweet, and I remember how you———"

"Arthur!"—she spoke fast and low—"Arthur, that letter was a forgery. She never wrote it. I———"

She stopped, for I had risen and flung her hands from me, and stood look-ing at her. God help me! I thought it was anger at the lie I felt. I know now it was only wounded vanity that smarted in me. That *I* should have been tricked, that *I* should have been deceived, that *I* should have been led on to make a fool of myself! That *I* should have married the woman who had befooled me! At that moment she was no longer the wife I adored—she was only a woman who had forged a letter and tricked me into marrying her.

I spoke; I denounced her; I said I would never speak to her again. I felt it was rather creditable in me to be so angry. I said I would have no more to do with a liar and forger.

I don't know whether I expected her to creep to my knees and implore for-giveness. I think I had some vague idea that I could by-and-by consent with dig-nity to forgive and forget. I did not mean what I said. No, no; I did not mean a word of it. While I was saying it I was longing for her to weep and fall at my feet, that I might raise her and hold her in my arms again.

But she did not fall at my feet; she stood quietly looking at me.

"Arthur," she said, as I paused for breath, "let me explain—she—I———"

"There is nothing to explain," I said hotly, still with that foolish sense of there being something rather noble in my indignation, as one feels when one calls one's self a miserable sinner. "You are a liar and forger, and that is enough for me. I will never speak to you again. You have wrecked my life——"

"Do you mean that?" she said, interrupting me, and leaning forward to look at me. Tears lay on her cheeks, but she was not crying now.

I hesitated. I longed to take her in my arms and say—"Lay your head here, my darling, and cry here, and know how I love you."

But instead I kept silence.

"*Do* you mean it?" she persisted.

Then she put her hand on my arm. I longed to clasp it and draw her to me.

Instead, I shook it off, and said—

"Mean it? Yes—of course I mean it. Don't touch me, please! You have ruined my life."

She turned away without a word, went into our room, and shut the door.

I longed to follow her, to tell her that if there was anything to forgive I forgave it.

Instead, I went out on the beach, and walked away under the cliffs.

The moonlight and the solitude, however, presently brought me to a better mind. Whatever she had done had been done for love of me—I knew that. I would go home and tell her so—tell her that whatever she had done she was my dearest life, my heart's one treasure. True, my ideal of her was shattered, but, even as she was, what was the whole world of women compared to her? I hurried back, but in my resentment and evil temper I had walked far, and the way back was very long. I had been parted from her for three hours by the time I opened the door of the little house where we lodged. The house was dark and very still. I slipped off my shoes and crept up the narrow stairs, and opened the door of our room quite softly. Perhaps she would have cried herself to sleep, and I would lean over her and waken her with my kisses and beg her to forgive me. Yes, it had come to that now.

I went into the room—I went towards the bed. She was not there. She was not in the room, as one glance showed me. She was not in the house, as I knew in two minutes. When I had wasted a priceless hour in searching the town for her, I found a note on the dressing-table—

"Good-bye! Make the best of what is left of your life. I will spoil it no more."

She was gone, utterly gone. I rushed to town by the earliest morning train, only to find that her people knew nothing of her. Advertisement failed. Only a tramp said he had met a white lady on the cliff, and a fisherman brought me a handkerchief marked with her name that he had found on the beach.

I searched the country far and wide, but I had to go back to London at last, and the months went by. I won't say much about those months, because even the memory of that suffering turns me faint and sick at heart. The police and detectives and the Press failed me utterly. Her friends could not help me, and were, moreover, wildly indignant with me, especially her brother, now living very happily with my first love.

I don't know how I got through those long weeks and months. I tried to write; I tried to read; I tried to live the life of a reasonable human being. But it was impossible. I could not endure the companionship of my kind. Day and night I almost saw her face—almost heard her voice. I took long walks in the country, and her figure was always just round the next turn of the road—in the next glade of the wood. But I never quite saw her—never quite heard her. I believe I was not altogether sane at that time. At last, one morning as I was setting out for one of those long walks that had no goal but weariness, I met a telegraph boy, and took the red envelope from his hand.

On the pink paper inside was written—

"Come to me at once. I am dying. You must come.—Ida.—Apinshaw Farm, Mellor, Derbyshire."

There was a train at twelve to Marple, the nearest station. I took it. I tell you there are some things that cannot be written about. My life for those long months was one of them, that journey was another. What had her life been for those months? That question troubled me, as one is troubled in every nerve at the sight of a surgical operation or a wound inflicted on a being dear to one. But the over-mastering sensation was joy—intense, unspeakable joy. She was alive! I should see her again. I took out the telegram and looked at it: "I am dying." I simply did not believe it. She could not die till she had seen me. And if she had lived all those months without me, she could live now, when I was with her again, when she knew of the hell I had endured apart from her, and the heaven of our meeting. She must live. I would not let her die.

There was a long drive over bleak hills. Dark, jolting, infinitely wearisome. At last we stopped before a long, low building, where one or two lights gleamed faintly. I sprang out.

The door opened. A blaze of light made me blink and draw back. A woman was standing in the doorway.

"Art thee Arthur Marsh?" she said.

"Yes."

"Then, th'art ower late. She's dead."

II.

I went into the house, walked to the fire, and held out my hands to it mechanically, for, though the night was May, I was cold to the bone. There were some folks standing round the fire and lights flickering. Then an old woman came forward with the northern instinct of hospitality.

"Thou'rt tired," she said, "and mazed-like. Have a sup o' tea."

I burst out laughing. It was too funny. I had travelled two hundred miles to see *her*, and she was dead, and they offered me tea. They drew back from me as if I had been a wild beast, but I could not stop laughing. Then a hand was laid on my shoulder, and someone led me into a dark room, lighted a lamp, set me in a chair, and sat down opposite me. It was a bare parlour, coldly furnished with rush chairs and much-polished tables and presses. I caught my breath, and grew suddenly grave, and looked at the woman who sat opposite me.

"I was Miss Ida's nurse," said she, "and she told me to send for you. Who are you?"

"Her husband——"

The woman looked at me with hard eyes, where intense surprise struggled with resentment. "Then, may God forgive you!" she said. "What you've done I don't know; but it'll be 'ard work forgivin' *you*—even for *Him*!"

"Tell me," I said, "my wife——"

"Tell you?" The bitter contempt in the woman's tone did not hurt me; what was it to the self-contempt that had gnawed my heart all these months? "Tell you? Yes, I'll tell you. Your wife was that ashamed of you, she never so much as told me she was married. She let me think anything I pleased sooner than that. She just come 'ere an' she said, 'Nurse, take care of me, for I am in mortal trouble. And don't let them know where I am,' says she. An' me bein' well married to an honest man, and well-to-do here, I was able to do it, by the blessing."

"Why didn't you send for me before?" It was a cry of anguish wrung from me.

"I'd *never* 'a sent for you—it was *her* doin'. Oh, to think as God A'mighty's made men able to measure out such-like pecks o' trouble for us womenfolk!

Young man, I dunno what you did to 'er to make 'er leave you; but it muster bin something cruel, for she loved the ground you walked on. She useter sit day after day, a-lookin' at your picture an' talkin' to it an' kissin' of it, when she thought I wasn't takin' no notice, and cryin' till she made me cry too. She useter cry all night 'most. An' one day, when I tells 'er to pray to God to 'elp 'er through 'er trouble, she outs with *your* putty face on a card, she doez, an', says she, with her poor little smile, 'That's my god, Nursey,' she says."

"Don't!" I said feebly, putting out my hands to keep off the torture; "not any more, not now."

"*Don't?*" she repeated. She had risen and was walking up and down the room with clasped hands—"don't, indeed! No, I won't; but I shan't forget you! I tell you I've had you in my prayers time and again, when I thought you'd made a light-o'-love o' my darling. I shan't drop you outer them now I know she was your own wedded wife as you chucked away when you'd tired of her, and left 'er to eat 'er 'art out with longin' for you. Oh! I pray to God above us to pay you scot and lot for all you done to 'er! You killed my pretty. The price will be required of you, young man, even to the uttermost farthing! O God in heaven, make him suffer! Make him feel it!"

She stamped her foot as she passed me. I stood quite still; I bit my lip till I tasted the blood hot and salt on my tongue.

"She was nothing to you!" cried the woman, walking faster up and down between the rush chairs and the table; "any fool can see that with half an eye. You didn't love her, so you don't feel nothin' now; but some day you'll care for someone, and then you shall know what she felt—if there's any justice in heaven!"

I, too, rose, walked across the room, and leaned against the wall. I heard her words without understanding them.

"Can't you feel *nothin*? Are you mader stone? Come an' look at 'er lyin' there so quiet. She don't fret arter the likes o' you no more now. She won't sit no more a-lookin' outer winder an' sayin' nothin'—only droppin' 'er tears one by one, slow, slow on her lap. Come an' see 'er; come an' see what you done to my pretty—an' then ye can go. Nobody wants you 'ere. *She* don't want you now. But p'r'aps you'd like to see 'er safe underground fust? I'll be bound you'll put a big slab on 'er—to make sure *she* don't rise again."

I turned on her. Her thin face was white with grief and impotent rage. Her claw-like hands were clenched.

"Woman," I said, "have mercy!"

She paused, and looked at me.

"Eh?" she said.

"Have mercy!" I said again.

"Mercy? You should 'a thought o' that before. You 'adn't no mercy on 'er. She loved you—she died lovin' you. An' if I wasn't a Christian woman, I'd kill you for it—like the rat you are! That I would, though I 'ad to swing for it arterwards."

I caught the woman's hands and held them fast, in spite of her resistance.

"Don't you understand?" I said savagely. "We loved each other. She died loving me. I have to live loving her. And it's *her* you pity. I tell you it was all a mistake—a stupid, stupid mistake. Take me to her, and for pity's sake let me be left alone with her."

She hesitated; then said in a voice only a shade less hard—

"Well, come along, then."

We moved towards the door. As she opened it a faint, weak cry fell on my ear. My heart stood still.

"What's that?" I asked, stopping on the threshold.

"Your child," she said shortly.

That, too! Oh, my love! oh, my poor love! All these long months!

"She allus said she'd send for you when she'd got over her trouble," the woman said as we climbed the stairs. "'I'd like him to see his little baby, nurse,' she says; 'our little baby. It'll be all right when the baby's born,' she says. 'I know he'll come to me then. You'll see.' And I never said nothin'—not thinkin' you'd come if she was your leavins, and not dreamin' as you could be 'er husband an' could stay away from 'er a hour—her bein' as she was. Hush!"

She drew a key from her pocket and fitted it to the lock. She opened the door and I followed her in. It was a large, dark room, full of old-fashioned furniture. There were wax candles in brass candlesticks and a smell of lavender.

The big four-post bed was covered with white.

"My lamb—my poor pretty lamb!" said the woman, beginning to cry for the first time as she drew back the sheet. "Don't she look beautiful?"

I stood by the bedside. I looked down on my wife's face. Just so I had seen it lie on the pillow beside me in the early morning when the wind and the dawn came up from beyond the sea. She did not look like one dead. Her lips were still red, and it seemed to me that a tinge of colour lay on her cheek. It seemed to me, too, that if I kissed her she would wake, and put her slight hand on my neck, and lay her cheek against mine—and that we should tell each other everything, and weep together, and understand and be comforted.

So I stooped and laid my lips to hers as the old nurse stole from the room.

But the red lips were like marble, and she did not wake. She will not wake now ever any more.

I tell you again there are some things that cannot be written.

III.

I lay that night in a big room filled with heavy, dark furniture, in a great four-poster hung with heavy, dark curtains—a bed the counterpart of that other bed from whose side they had dragged me at last.

They fed me, I believe, and the old nurse was kind to me. I think she saw now that it is not the dead who are to be pitied most.

I lay at last in the big, roomy bed, and heard the household noises grow fewer and die out, the little wail of my child sounding latest. They had brought the child to me, and I had held it in my arms, and bowed my head over its tiny face and frail fingers. I did not love it then. I told myself it had cost me her life. But my heart told me that it was I who had done that. The tall clock at the stairhead sounded the hours—eleven, twelve, one, and still I could not sleep. The room was dark and very still.

I had not been able to look at my life quietly. I had been full of the intoxica-tion of grief—a real drunkenness, more merciful than the calm that comes after.

Now I lay still as the dead woman in the next room, and looked at what was left of my life. I lay still, and thought, and thought, and thought. And in those hours I tasted the bitterness of death. It must have been about two that I first became aware of a slight sound that was not the ticking of the clock. I say I first became aware, and yet I knew perfectly that I had heard that sound more than once before, and had yet determined not to hear it, *because it came from the next room*—the room where the corpse lay.

And I did not wish to hear that sound, because I knew it meant that I was nervous—miserably nervous—a coward and a brute. It meant that I, having killed my wife as surely as though I had put a knife in her breast, had now sunk so low as to be afraid of her dead body—the dead body that lay in the room next to mine. The heads of the beds were placed against the same wall; and from that wall I had fancied I heard slight, slight, almost inaudible sounds. So when I say that I became aware of them I mean that I at last heard a sound so distinct as to leave no room for doubt or question. It brought me to a sitting position in the bed, and the drops of sweat gathered heavily on my forehead and fell on my cold hands as I held my breath and listened.

I don't know how long I sat there—there was no further sound—and at last my tense muscles relaxed, and I fell back on the pillow.

"You fool!" I said to myself; "dead or alive, is she not your darling, your heart's heart? Would you not go near to die of joy if she came to you? Pray God to let her spirit come back and tell you she forgives you!"

"I wish she would come," myself answered in words, while every fibre of my body and mind shrank and quivered in denial.

I struck a match, lighted a candle, and breathed more freely as I looked at the polished furniture—the commonplace details of an ordinary room. Then I thought of her, lying alone, so near me, so quiet under the white sheet. She was dead; she would not wake or move. But suppose she did move? Suppose she turned back the sheet and got up, and walked across the floor and turned the door-handle?

As I thought it, I heard—plainly, unmistakably heard—the door of the chamber of death open slowly—I heard slow steps in the passage, slow, heavy steps—I heard the touch of hands on my door outside, uncertain hands, that felt for the latch.

Sick with terror, I lay clenching the sheet in my hands.

I knew well enough what would come in when that door opened—that door on which my eyes were fixed. I dreaded to look, yet I dared not turn away my eyes. The door opened slowly, slowly, slowly, and the figure of my dead wife came in. It came straight towards the bed, and stood at the bed-foot in its white grave-clothes, with the white bandage under its chin. There was a scent of lavender. Its eyes were wide open and looked at me with love unspeakable.

I could have shrieked aloud.

My wife spoke. It was the same dear voice that I had loved so to hear, but it was very weak and faint now; and now I trembled as I listened.

"You aren't afraid of me, darling, are you, though I am dead? I heard all you said to me when you came, but I couldn't answer. But now I've come back from the dead to tell you. I wasn't really so bad as you thought me. Elvire had told me she loved Oscar. I only wrote the letter to make it easier for you. I was too proud to tell you when you were so angry, but I am not proud any more now. You'll love me again now, won't you, now I'm dead? One always forgives dead people."

The poor ghost's voice was hollow and faint. Abject terror paralyzed me. I could answer nothing.

"Say you forgive me," the thin, monotonous voice went on; "say you love me again."

I had to speak. Coward as I was, I did manage to stammer—

"Yes; I love you. I have always loved you, God help me!"

The sound of my own voice reassured me, and I ended more firmly than I began. The figure by the bed swayed a little unsteadily.

"I suppose," she said wearily, "you would be afraid, now I am dead, if I came round to you and kissed you?"

She made a movement as though she would have come to me.

Then I did shriek aloud, again and again, and covered my face with the sheet, and wound it round my head and body, and held it with all my force.

There was a moment's silence. Then I heard my door close, and then a sound of feet and of voices, and I heard something heavy fall. I disentangled my head from the sheet. My room was empty. Then reason came back to me. I leaped from the bed.

"Ida, my darling, come back! I am not afraid! I love you! Come back! Come back!"

I sprang to my door and flung it open. Someone was bringing a light along the passage. On the floor, outside the door of the death-chamber, was a huddled heap—the corpse, in its grave-clothes. Dead, dead, dead.

She is buried in Mellor churchyard, and there is no stone over her.

Now, whether it was catalepsy—as the doctors said—or whether my love came back even from the dead to me who loved her, I shall never know; but this I know—that, if I had held out my arms to her as she stood at my bed-foot—if I had said, "Yes, even from the grave, my darling—from hell itself, come back, come back to me!"—if I had had room in my coward's heart for anything but the unreasoning terror that killed love in that hour, I should not now be here alone. I shrank from her—I feared her—I would not take her to my heart. And now she will not come to me any more.

Why do I go on living?

You see, there is the child. It is four years old now, and it has never spoken and never smiled.

IN THE SÉANCE ROOM*

Lettice Galbraith

Dr. Valentine Burke sat alone by the fire. He had finished his rounds, and no patient had disturbed his post-prandial reflections. The house was very quiet, for the servants had gone to bed, and only the occasional rattle of a passing cab and the light patter of the rain on the window-panes broke the silence of the night. The cheerful glow of the fire and the soft light from the yellow-shaded lamp contrasted pleasantly with the dreary fog which filled the street outside. There were spirit-decanters on the table, flanked by a siphon and a box of choice cigars. Valentine Burke liked his creature comforts. The world and the flesh held full measure of attraction for him, but he did not care about working for his *menus plaisirs*.

The ordinary routine of his profession bored him. That he might eventually succeed as a ladies' doctor was tolerably certain. For a young man with little influence and less money, he was doing remarkably well; but Burke was ambitious, and he had a line of his own. He dabbled in psychics, and had written an article on the future of hypnotism, which had attracted considerable attention. He was a strong magnetiser, and offered no objection to semi-private exhibitions of his powers. In many drawing-rooms he was already regarded as the apostle of the coming revolution which is to substitute disintegration of matter and cerebral precipitation for the present system of the parcels mail and telegraphic communication. In that section of society which interests itself in occultism Burke saw his way to making a big success. Meanwhile, as man cannot live on adulation alone, the doctor had a living to get, and he had no intention whatever of getting it by the labour of his hands. He was an astute young man, who knew how to invest his capital to the best advantage. His good looks were his capital, and he was about to invest them in a wealthy marriage. The fates had certainly been propitious when they brought Miss Elma Lang into the charmed circle of the Society for the Revival of Eastern Mysticism. Miss Lang was

---

* "In the Séance Room" appeared in Galbraith's collection *New Ghost Stories* (London: Ward, Lock, 1893). The current text is based on this edition. Obvious typographical errors and inconsistencies have been silently corrected.

an orphan. She had full control of her fortune of thirty thousand pounds. She was young, sufficiently pretty, and extremely susceptible. Burke saw his chance, and went for it, to such good purpose that before a month had passed his engagement to the heiress was announced, and the wedding-day within measurable distance. There were several other candidates for Miss Lang's hand, but it soon became evident that the doctor was first favourite. The gentlemen who devoted themselves to occultism for the most part despised physical attractions; their garments were fearfully and wonderfully made. They were careless as to the arrangement of their hair. Beside them, Valentine Burke, handsome, well set up, and admirably turned out, showed to the very greatest advantage. Elma Lang adored him. She was never tired of admiring him. She was lavish of pretty tokens of her regard. Her photographs, in costly frames, were scattered about his room, and on his hand glittered the single-stone diamond ring which had been her betrothal gift.

He smiled pleasantly as he watched the fire-light glinting from the many-coloured facets. "I have been lucky," he said aloud; "I pulled that through very neatly. Just in time, too, for my credit would not stand another year. I ought to be all right now if——." He broke off abruptly, and the smile died away. "If it were not for that other unfortunate affair! What a fool—what a d—d fool I was not to let the girl alone, and what a fool she was to trust me! Why could she not have taken better care of herself? Why could not the old man have looked after her? He made row enough over shutting the stable-door when the horse was gone. It was cleverly managed though. I think even *ce cher papa* exonerates me from any participation in her disappearance; and fate seems to be playing into my hand too. That body turning up just now is a stroke of luck. I wonder who the poor devil really is?"

He felt for his pocket-book, and took out a newspaper cutting. It was headed in large type, "Mysterious Disappearance of a Young Lady.—The body found yesterday by the police in Muddlesham Harbour is believed to be that of Miss Katharine Greaves, whose mysterious disappearance in January last created so great a sensation. It will be remembered that Miss Greaves, who was a daughter of a well-known physician at Templeford, Worcestershire, had gone to Muddlesham on a visit to her married sister, from whose house she suddenly disappeared. Despite the most strenuous efforts on the part of her distracted family, backed by the assistance of able detectives, her fate has up to the present remained enshrouded in mystery. On the recovery of the body yesterday the Muddlesham police at once communicated with the relations of Miss Greaves, by whom the clothing was identified. It is now supposed that the unhappy girl threw herself into the harbour during a fit of temporary insanity, resulting, it is believed, from an unfortunate love affair."

Valentine Burke read the paragraph through carefully, and replaced it in the pocket-book with a cynical smile.

"How exquisitely credulous are the police, and the relatives, and the noble British public. Poor Kitty is practically dead—to the world. What a pity——" He hesitated, and stared into the blazing coals. "It would save so much trouble," he went on after a pause, "and I hate trouble."

His fingers were playing absently with a letter from which he had taken the slip of printed paper—an untidy letter, blotted and smeared, and hastily written on poor, thin paper. He looked at it once or twice and tossed it into the fire. The note-sheet shrivelled and curled over, dropping on to the hearth, where it lay smouldering. A hot cinder had fallen out of the grate, and the doctor, stretching out his foot, kicked the letter closer to the live coal. Little red sparks crept like glowworms along the scorched edges flickered and died out. The paper would not ignite; it was damp—damp with a woman's tears. "I was a fool," he murmured, with conviction. "It was not good enough, and it might have ruined me." He turned to the spirit-stand and replenished his glass, measuring the brandy carefully. "I don't know that I am out of the wood yet," he went on, as he filled up the tumbler with soda-water. "The money is running short, and women are so d—d inconsiderate. If Kitty were to take it into her head to turn up here it would be the——" The sentence remained unfinished, cut short by a sound from below. Someone had rung the night-bell.

Burke set down the glass and bent forward, listening intently. The ring, timid, almost deprecating, was utterly unlike the usual imperative summons for medical aid. Following immediately on his outspoken thoughts, it created an uncomfortable impression of coming danger. He felt certain that it was not a patient; and if it were not a patient, who was it? There was a balcony to the window. He stepped quietly out and leaned over the railing. By the irregular flicker of the street-lamp he could make out the dark figure of a woman on the steps beneath, and through the patter of the falling rain he fancied he caught the sound of a suppressed sob. With a quick glance, to assure himself that no one was in sight, the doctor ran downstairs and opened the door. A swirl of rain blew into the lighted hall. The woman was leaning against one of the pillars apparently unconscious. Burke touched her shoulder. "What are you doing here?" he asked sharply. At the sound of his voice she uttered a little cry and made a sudden step forward, stumbling over the threshold, and falling heavily against him.

"Val, Val," she cried, despairingly, "I thought I should never find you. Take me home, take me home. I am so tired—and, oh, so frightened!"

The last word died away in a wailing sob, then her hands relaxed their clinging hold and dropped nervelessly at her side.

In an emergency Dr. Burke acted promptly. He shut the outer door, and gathering up the fainting girl in his arms, carried her into the consulting-room, and laid her on the sofa. There was no touch of tenderness in his handling of the unconscious form. He had never cared much about her, when at her best, dainty in figure and fair of face; he had made love to her, *pour passer le temps*, in the dullness of a small country town. She had met him more than half way, and almost before his caprice was gratified he was weary of her. Her very devotion nauseated him. He looked at her now with a shudder of repulsion. The gaslight flared coldly on the white face, drawn by pain and misery. All its pretty youthfulness had vanished. The short hair, uncurled by the damp night air, straggled over the thin forehead. There were lines about the closed eyes and the drooping corners of the mouth. The skin was strained tightly over the cheek-bones and looked yellow, like discoloured wax. His eyes noted every defect of face and figure, as he stood wondering what he should do with her. He knew, no one better, how quickly the breath of scandal can injure a professional man. Once let the real story of his relations with Katharine Greaves get wind and his career would be practically ruined. He began to realise the gravity of the situation. Two futures lay before him. The one, bright with the sunshine of love and prosperity; the other darkened by poverty and disgrace. He pictured himself the husband of Elma Lang, with all the advantages accruing to the possessor of a charming wife and a large fortune, and he cursed fate which had sent this wreck of womanhood to stand between him and happiness. By this time she had partially recovered, and her eyes opened with the painful upward roll common to nervous patients when regaining consciousness. With her dishevelled hair and rain-soaked garments, she had all the appearance of a dead body. The sight, horrible as it was, fascinated Burke. He turned up the gas, twisting the chandelier so as to throw a full light on the girl's face.

"She looks as though she were drowned," he thought. "When she is really dead she will look like that." The idea took possession of his mind. "If she were dead, if only she were really dead!"

Who can trust the discretion of a wronged and forsaken woman, but—the dead tell no tales. If only she were dead! The words repeated themselves again and again, beating into his brain like the heavy strokes of a hammer. Why should she not die? Her life was over, a spoiled, ruined thing. There was nothing before her but shame and misery. She would be better dead. Why (he laughed suddenly a hard, mirthless laugh), she *was* dead already. Her body had been found by the police, identified by her own relations. She was supposed to be drowned, so why not make the supposition a reality? A curious light flashed into the doctor's handsome face. A woman seeing him at that moment would have hesitated before trusting her life in his hands. He looked at his unwelcome visitor with an evil smile.

She had come round now and was crouched in the corner of the sofa sobbing and shivering.

"Don't be angry with me, Val, please don't be angry. I waited till I had only just enough money for my ticket, and I dare not stay there any longer. It is so lonely, and you never come to see me now. It is ten weeks since you were down, and you won't answer my letters. I was so frightened all alone. I began to think you were getting tired of me. Of course I know it is all nonsense. You love me as much as you ever did. It is only that you are so busy and hate writing letters." She paused, waiting for some reassuring words, but he did not answer, only watched her with cold, steady eyes.

"Did you see the papers," she went on, with chattering teeth. "They think I am dead. Ever since I read it I have had such dreadful thoughts. I keep seeing myself drowned; I believe I am going to die, Val—and I don't want to die. I am so—so frightened. I thought you would take me in your arms and comfort me like you used to do, and I should feel safe. Oh, why don't you speak to me? Why do you look at me like that? Val, dear, don't do it, *don't* do it, I cannot bear it."

Her great terrified eyes were fixed on his, fascinated by his steady, unflinching gaze. She was trembling violently. Her words came with difficulty, in short gasps.

"You have never said you were glad to see me. It is true, then, that you don't love me any more. You are tired of me, and you will not marry me now. What shall I do? what shall I do? No one cares for me, no one wants me, and there is nothing left for me but to die."

Still no answer. There was a long silence while their eyes met in that fixed stare—his cold, steady, dominating, hers flinching and striving vainly to withstand the power of the stronger will. In a few moments the unequal struggle had ended. The girl sat stiff and erect, her hand grasping the arm of the sofa. The light of consciousness had died out of the blue eyes, leaving them fixed and glassy. Burke crossed the floor and stood in front of her.

"Where is your luggage?" he asked, authoritatively.

She answered in a dull, mechanical way, "At the station."

"Have you kept anything marked with your own name—any of my letters?"

"No, nothing—there."

"You *have* kept some of my letters. Where are they?"

"Here." Her hand sought vaguely for her pocket.

"Give them to me—all of them."

Mechanically she obeyed him, holding out three envelopes, after separating them carefully from her purse and handkerchief.

"Give me the other things." He opened the purse. Besides a few shillings, it contained only a visiting-card, on which an address had been written in pencil. The doctor tore the card across and tossed it into the fireplace. Then his eyes fastened on those of the girl before him. Very slowly he bent forward and whispered a few words in her ear, repeating them again and again. The abject terror visible in her face would have touched any heart but that of the man in whose path she stood. No living soul, save the "sensitive" on whom he was experimenting, heard those words, but they were registered by a higher power than that of the criminal court, damning evidence to be produced one day against the man who had prostituted his spiritual gift to mean and selfish ends.

In the grey light of the chilly November morning a park-keeper, near the Regent's Canal, was startled by a sudden, piercing shriek. Hurrying in the direction of the sound, he saw, through leafless branches, a figure struggling in the black water. The park-keeper was a plucky fellow, whose courage had gained more than one recognition from the Humane Society, and he began to run towards the spot where the dark form had been, but before he had covered ten yards of ground rapid footsteps gained on his and a man shot past him. "Someone in the canal," he shouted as he ran. "I think it is a woman. You had better get help."

"He was a good plucky one," the park-keeper averred, when a few days later he retailed the story to a select circle of friends at the bar of the "Regent's Arms," where the inquest had been held. "Not that I'd have been behindhand, but my wind ain't what it was, and he might have been shot out of a catapult. He was off with his coat and into the water before you could say Jack Robinson. Twice I thought he had her safe enough, and twice she pulled him under; the third time, blest if I thought they were coming up any more at all. Then the doctor chap, he comes to the surface dead-beat, but the girl in his arms."

"'I'm afraid she's gone,' he says, when I took her from him, 'but we won't lose time,' and he set to and carried out all the instructions for recovering the apparently drowned while I went for some brandy. It wasn't a bit of use. The young woman were as dead as a doornail. 'If she'd only have kept quiet, I might have saved her,' he says, quite sorrowful like, 'but she struggled so,' and sure enough his hands were regularly torn and bruised where she'd gripped him."

Dr. Burke and the park-keeper were the chief witnesses at the inquest. There were no means of identifying the dead woman. The jury returned a verdict of *felo de se*, and the coroner complimented the doctor on his courageous attempt to rescue the poor outcast.

The newspapers, too, gave him a nice little paragraph, headed, "Determined Suicide in Regent's Park. Gallant conduct of a well-known physician;" and Elma Lang's dark eyes filled with fond and happy tears as she read her lover's praises.

"You are so brave, Val, so good," she cried, "and I am so proud of you; but you ran a horrible risk."

"Yes," he answered, gravely, "I thought once it was all up with me. That poor girl nearly succeeded in drowning the pair of us. Still, there wasn't much in it, you know; any other fellow would have done the same."

"No, they would not. It is no use trying to pretend you are not a hero, Val, because you are. How awful it must have been when she clung to you so desperately. It might have cost you your life."

"It cost me my ring," he replied, ruefully. "It is lying at the bottom of the canal at this moment, unless some adventurous fish has swallowed it—your first gift."

"What does it matter," she answered, impulsively, "I can give you another to-morrow. What does anything matter since you are safe?"

Burke took her in his arms, and kissed the pretty upturned face. She was his now, bought with the price of another woman's life. Bah! he wanted to forget the clutch of those stiffening fingers and the glazed awful stare of the dead eyes through the water.

"Let us drop the subject," he said, gently. "It is not a pleasant one, and, as you say, nothing matters since I am safe"——he added under his breath, "quite safe *now*."

* * *

The carriage stood at the door. In the drawing-room Mrs. Burke was waiting for her husband. She had often waited for the doctor during the four years which had elapsed since their marriage. Those four years had seen to a great extent the fulfilment of Burke's ambition. He had money. He was popular, sought after, an acknowledged leader of the new school of Philosophy, an authority on psychic phenomena, and the idol of the "smart" women who played with the fashionable theories and talked glibly on subjects the very A B C of which was far beyond their feeble comprehension. Socially, Dr. Burke was an immense success. If, as a husband, he fell short of Elma's expectations, she never admitted the fact. She made an admirable wife, interesting herself in his studies, and assisting him materially in his literary work. Outwardly, they were a devoted couple. The world knew nothing of the indefinable barrier which held husband and wife apart; of a certain vague distrust which had crept into the woman's heart, bred of an instinctive feeling that her husband was not what he seemed to be. Something, she knew not what, lay between them. Her quick perceptions told her that he was always acting a part. She held in her hand a little sheaf of papers, notes that she had prepared for him on the series of *séances*, which for a month past had been the talk of the town. A medium of extraordinary power had flashed like a meteor into the firmament of London society. Phenomena of the most startling kind had baffled alike the explanations of both scientist and occultist. Spiritualism was triumphant. A test committee had been formed, of which Dr. Burke was unanimously elected president, but so far the attempts to expose the alleged frauds had not been attended with any success.

It was to Mdme. Delphine's house that the Burkes were going to-night. The *séance* commenced at ten, and the hands of the clock already pointed to a quarter to that hour, when the doctor hurried into the room.

"Ready?" he said. "Come along then. Where are the notes?"

He glanced hastily through them as he went downstairs.

"Falconer and I have been there all the afternoon," he explained as they drove off. "I had only just time to get something to eat at the club before I dressed. We have taken the most elaborate precautions. If something cannot be proved to-night——" He paused.

"Well?" she said, anxiously.

"We shall be the laughing-stock of London," he concluded, emphatically.

"What do you really think of it?"

"Humbug, of course; but the difficulty is to prove it."

"Mrs. Thirlwall declares that the fifth appearance last night was undoubtedly her husband. I saw her today; she was quite overcome."

"Mrs. Thirlwall is an hysterical fool."

"But your theory admitted the possibility of materialising the intense mental——"

Burke leaned back in the carriage, laughing softly.

"My dear child, I had to say something."

"Valentine," she cried, sorrowfully, "is there no truth in anything you say or write? Do you believe in nothing?"

"Certainly. I believe in matter and myself, also that the many fools exist for the benefit of a minority with brains. When I see any reason to alter my belief, I shall not hesitate to do so. If, for instance, I am convinced that I see with my material eyes a person whom I know to be dead, I will become a convert to spiritualism. But I shall never see it."

The drawing-room was filled when they arrived at Mdme. Delphine's. Seats had been kept for the doctor and his wife. There was a short whispered consultation between Burke and his colleagues, the usual warning from the medium that the audience must conform to the rules of the *séance*, and the business of the evening began in the customary style. Musical instruments sounded in different parts of the room, light fingers touched the faces of the sitters. Questions written on slips of paper and placed in a sealed cabinet received answers from the spirit world, which the inquirers admitted to be correct. The medium's assistant handed one of these blank slips to Burke, requesting him to fill it up.

It struck the doctor that if he were to ask some question the answer to which he did not himself know, but could afterwards verify, he would guard against the possibility of playing into the hands of an adroit thought-reader. He accordingly wrote on the paper, "What was I doing this time four years ago? Give the initials of my companions, if any."

He had not the vaguest idea as to where exactly he had been on the date in question, but a reference to the rough diary he always kept would verify or disprove the answer.

The folded slip was sealed and placed in the cabinet. In due time the medium declared the replies were ready. The cabinet was opened, and the slips, numbered in the order in which they had been given in, were returned to their owners. Burke noticed that there were no fresh folds in his paper, and the seal was of course unbroken. He opened it, and as his eye fell on the writing he gave a slight start, and glanced sharply at the medium. Beneath his query was written in ink that was scarcely yet dry, "On Wednesday, November, 17, 1885, you were at No. 63, Abbey Road. I only was with you. You hypnotised me.—K. G." The handwriting was that of Katharine Greaves.

The doctor was staggered. In the multiplied interests and distractions of his daily life he had completely forgotten the date of that tragic visit. He tried to recall the exact day of the month and week. He remembered now that it was on a Wednesday, and this was Monday. Calculating the odd days for the leap year, 1888, that would bring it to Monday—Monday, the 17th. Four years ago to-night Kitty had been alive. She was dead now, and yet here before him was a paper written in her hand. He sat staring at the characters, lost in thought. The familiar writing brought back with irresistible force the memory of that painful interview. It suggested another and very serious danger. Burke did not believe for a moment that the answer to his question had been dictated by the disembodied spirit of his victim. He was racking his brains to discover how his secret might possibly have leaked out, who this woman could be who knew, and traded on her knowledge, of that dark passage in his life which he had believed to be hidden from all the world. Was it merely a bow drawn at a venture, which had chanced to strike the one weak place in his armour, or was it deliberately planned with a view to extorting money?

So deeply was he wrapped in his reflections, that the manifestations went on around him unheeded. The dark curtain which screened off a portion of the room divided, and a white-robed child stepped out. It was instantly recognised by one of the sitters—a nervous, highly-strung woman, whose passionate entreaties that her dead darling would return to earth fairly harrowed the feelings of the listeners. Other manifestations followed. The audience were becoming greatly excited. Burke sat indifferent to it all, his eyes fixed on the writing before him, till his wife touched him gently.

"What is the matter, Val?" she whispered, trying to read the paper over his shoulder. "Is your answer correct?"

He turned on her sharply, crushing the message in his hand. "No," he said audibly. "It is a gross imposture. There was no such person."

"Hush." She laid a restraining hand on his arm. "Do not speak so loudly. That is a point in our favour, anyway. Mr. Falconer has proposed a fresh test. He has asked if a material object, something that had been lost at any time, you know, can be restored by the spirits. Madame returned a favourable answer. Mr. Falconer could not think of anything at the moment, but I had a brilliant inspiration. I told him to ask for your diamond ring—the ring you lost when you tried to save that poor girl's life."

Burke rose to his feet, then recollecting himself, sat down again and tried to pull himself together. There was nothing in it. If this Madame Delphine was really acquainted with the facts of his relations with Katharine Greaves she could not know its ghastly termination. He tried to reassure himself, but vainly. His nerve was deserting him, and his eyes roved vacantly round the semi-darkened room, as if in search of something. A sudden silence had fallen on the audience. A cold chill, like a draft of icy air, swept through the *séance* chamber. Mrs. Burke shivered from head to foot, and drew closer to her husband. Suddenly the stillness was broken by a shriek of horror. It issued from the lips of the medium, who, like a second Witch of Endor, saw more than she expected, and crouched terror-stricken in the chair to which she was secured by cords adjusted by the test committee. The presence which had appeared before the black curtain was no white-clad denizen of "summer-land," but a woman in dark, clinging garments—garments, to all appearance, dripping with water—a woman with wide-opened, glassy eyes, fixed in an unalterable stony stare. It was a ghastly sight. All the concentrated agony of a violent death was stamped on that awful face.

Of the twenty people who looked upon it, not one had power to move or speak.

Slowly the terrible thing glided forward, hardly touching the ground, one hand outstretched, and on the open palm a small, glittering object—a diamond ring!

It moved very slowly, and the second or so during which it traversed the space between the curtain and the seats of the audience seemed hours to the man who knew for whom it came.

Valentine Burke sat rigid. He was oblivious of the presence of spectators, hardly conscious of his own existence. Everything was swallowed up in a suspense too agonising for words, the fearful expectancy of what was about to happen. Nearer and nearer "it" came. Now it was close to him. He could feel the deathly dampness of its breath; those awful eyes were looking into his. The distorted lips parted—formed a single word. Was it the voice of a guilty conscience, or did that word really ring through and through the room—"Murderer!"

For a full minute the agony lasted, then something fell with a sharp click on the carpetless floor. The sound recalled the petrified audience to a consciousness of mundane things. They became aware that "it" was gone.

They moved furtively, glanced at each other—at last someone spoke. It was Mrs. Burke. She had vainly tried to attract her husband's attention, and now turned to Falconer, who sat next to her.

"Help me to get him away," she said.

The doctor alone had not stirred; his eyes were fixed as though he were still confronted by that unearthly presence.

Someone had turned up the gas. Two of the committee were releasing the medium, who was half dead with fright. Falconer unfastened the door, and sent a servant whom he met in the hall for a hansom.

When he returned to the *séance* room the doctor was still in the same position. It was some moments before he could be roused, but when once they succeeded in their efforts Burke's senses seemed to return. He rose directly, and prepared to accompany his wife. As they quitted their seats, Falconer's eyes fell on the diamond ring which lay unnoticed on the ground. He was going to pick it up, but someone caught his hand and stopped him.

"Leave it alone," said Mrs. Burke, in a horrified whisper. "For God's sake, don't touch it!"

Husband and wife drove home in silence. Silently the doctor dismissed the cab and opened the hall-door. The gas was burning brightly in the study. The servant had left on the side-table a tray with sandwiches, wine, and spirits. Burke poured out some brandy and tossed it off neat. His face was still rather white, otherwise he had quite recovered his usual composure.

Mrs. Burke loosened her cloak and dropped wearily into a chair by the fire. A hopeless despondency was visible in every line of her attitude. Once or twice the doctor looked at her, and opened his lips to speak. Then he thought better of it, and kept silence. Half an hour passed in this way. At last Burke lighted a candle and left the room. When he returned he carried in his hand a small bottle. He had completely regained his self-possession as he came over to his wife and scrutinised her troubled face.

"Have some wine," he said, "and then you had better go to bed. You look thoroughly done up."

"What is that?" She pointed to the bottle in his hand.

"A sleeping-draught. Merely a little morphia and bromide. I should advise you to take one, too. Frankly, to-night's performance was enough to try the strongest nerves. Mine require steadying by a good night's rest, and I do not intend risking an attack of insomnia."

She rose suddenly from her chair and clasped her hands on his arm.

"Val," she cried, piteously, "don't try to deceive me. Dear, I can bear anything if you will only trust me and tell me the truth. What is this thing which stands between us? What was the meaning of that awful sight?"

For a moment he hesitated; then he pulled himself together and answered lightly—

"My dear girl, you are unnerved, and I do not wonder at it. Let us forget it."

"I cannot, I cannot," she interrupted wildly. "I must know what it meant. I have always felt there was something. Valentine, I beseech you, by everything you hold sacred, tell me the truth now before it is too late. I could forgive you almost—almost anything, if you will tell me bravely; but do not leave me to find it out for myself."

"There is nothing to tell."

"You will not trust me?"

"I tell you there is nothing."

"That is your final answer?"

"Yes."

Without a word she left the room and went upstairs. Burke soon followed her. His nerves had been sufficiently shaken to make solitude undesirable. He smoked a cigar in his dressing-room, and took the sleeping-draught before going to bed. The effects of the opiate lasted for several hours. It was broad daylight when the doctor awoke. He felt weak and used up, and his head was splitting. He lay for a short time in that drowsy condition which is the border-land between sleeping and waking. Then he became conscious that his wife was not in the room. He looked at his watch, and saw that it was half-past nine. He waited a few minutes, expecting her to return, but she did not come. Presently he got up and drew back the window-curtains. As the full light streamed in, he was struck by a certain change in the appearance of the room. At first he was uncertain in what the change consisted, but gradually he realised that it lay in the absence of the usual feminine impedimenta. The dressing-table was shorn of its silver toilet accessories. One or two drawers were open and emptied of their contents. The writing-table was cleared, and his wife's dressing-case had disappeared from its usual place. Burke's first impulse was to ring for a servant and make inquiries, but as he stretched out his hand to the bell his eyes fell on a letter, conspicuously placed on the centre of a small table. It was addressed in Elma's handwriting. From that moment Burke knew that something had happened, and he was prepared for the worst. The letter was not long. It was written firmly, though pale-blue stains here and there indicated where the wet ink had been splashed by falling tears.

"When you read this," she wrote, "I shall have left you for ever. The only reparation in your power is to refrain from any attempt to follow me; indeed, you will hardly desire to do so, when I tell you that I know all. I said last night I could not endure the torture of uncertainty. My fears were so terrible that I felt I must know the truth or die. I implored you to trust me. You put me off with a lie. Was I to blame if I used against you a power which you yourself had taught me? In the last four hours I have heard from your own lips the whole story of Katharine Greaves. Every detail of that horrible tragedy you confessed unconsciously in your sleep, and I who loved you—Heaven knows how dearly!—have to endure the agony of knowing my husband to be a murderer, and that my wretched fortune supplied the motive for the crime. Thank God that I have no child to bear the curse of your sin, to inherit its father's nature! I hardly know what I am writing. The very ground seems to be cut away from under my feet. On every side I can see nothing but densest darkness, and the only thing that is left to us is death.—Your wretched wife, ELMA."

From the moment he opened the letter, Burke's decision was made. He possessed the exact admixture of physical courage and moral cowardice which induces a man worsted in the battle of life to end the conflict by removing himself from the arena. He had taken the best of the world's gifts, and there was nothing left worth having. His belief in a future life was too vague to cause him any uneasiness, and physically, fear was a word he did not understand. He quietly lighted his wife's letter with a match, and threw it into the fireless grate. He smoked a cigarette while he watched it burn, and carefully hid the charred ashes among the cinders. Then he fetched from his dressing-room a small polished box, unlocked it, and took out the revolver. It was loaded in all six chambers.

Burke leisurely finished his cigarette, and tossed the end away. He never hesitated a moment. He had no regret for the life he was leaving. As Elma had said, there was only one thing left for him to do, and—he did it.

THE HOUSE WHICH WAS RENT FREE*

G. M. Robins

It seemed an offer that I ought to accept, merely for the sake of the children. It would just make all the difference! If I had no rent, rates, or taxes to pay for the first year, it might be possible to make ends meet; for, by next year, those terrible debts would all be paid, and my own small income clear.

I was determined to pay off everything, at any cost; but the expenses of those operations, that illness, that death, had been greater than seemed possible to me in my ignorance, and had left us woefully crippled in our loneliness, Ruth, Lettice, and I.

Yet somehow, now that the house in Belgrave Square, and the shooting-box, and the yacht, were all things of the past, I breathed more freely; my widow's weeds were to me the outward signs of a freedom I had scarcely dared to hope for. Charles Preston was in his grave, and with him I could bury all the bitter thoughts of what he had made me suffer. Thank God, only I had known it. There is no need to speak of it to anyone now; the anguish and the struggles are over, and the deadly nightmare lest others beside myself should *have* to know. Peace to the dead!

I was touched that this offer of help should come from Sidney Locke, for in the ten years since my marriage I had never seen him. He had sent me a sumptuous wedding-present, but he had not been present at the wedding. I kept those pearls, when I sold with joy the jewels that Charles had lavished upon me, because they were the only thing I had which came from the only person I knew who remembered me in the old vicarage days. Sidney had been kind then. In fact, I used gleefully to think that he was jealous when Charles whirled me away behind his spanking grey horses, a bride of nineteen, her curly head completely turned by a wooing

---

* "The House Which Was Rent Free" was included as the Young Matron's story in the series 'The Relations and What They Related', which originally ran in *The Lady's Realm* from February to November 1902. Robins then published the stories as *The Relations and What They Related* (London: Hutchinson, 1902). A second edition was published by Mills & Boon in 1914. The current text is based on *The Lady's Realm* publication. Obvious typographical errors and inconsistencies have been silently corrected.

that took six weeks from first to last.

And now, after the ten years' silence, came Sidney's voice, speaking to me, as it were, out of the past.

"I am so grieved, as well as surprised, to learn that Preston has left you badly off. May an old friend make a suggestion? Since you and I were acquainted I have become a landed proprietor, and I have a pretty house in Dorsetshire which I should like to lend you, as I think you may for the present feel inclined to a quiet country life. The house is fairly well furnished, and not too large to be comfortable. If you could make use of it for a year or so, you would do me a great service, for a foolish tale of its being haunted has got about in the neighbourhood, and, ridiculous as it may seem in these days, I cannot let it. If you would go down and refute this nonsense by occupying the house I should hold myself greatly your debtor. I am sure you would be pleased with the neighbourhood, and the air is very fine."

He did not, could not know, this man who wrote to me, how much his offer meant, how low was my exchequer, how great the problem as to how Ruth, Lettice, myself, and old Darley, my nurse, were to be suitably housed and fed during the next twelve months. This remote spot was the very thing; we should want no new frocks, and food would be cheap and plentiful.

"Darley," I said, "it will be the saving of us."

"You're never going to accept a favour from a cast-off lover!" said the old woman indignantly.

"Darley, what do you mean? Mr. Locke was never my lover."

"Oh, wasn't he! Much you know about it," was the old body's anything but respectful reply.

"Besides," I went on with dignity, "the favour is a mutual one; I shall oblige Mr. Locke by living in his house, which is furnished and without a tenant. Nobody is likely to take such a house at this time of the year. I shall accept this offer on condition that the house still remains "To Let," and that we turn out for any permanent tenant who may appear."

I did not tell Darley of the foolish local superstition; elderly country women are often superstitious.

There was no caretaker at Dennismore Hall, so I sent down my ex-coachman and his wife to make ready for our arrival. They had been long in my service, and were people I could depend upon. I felt sure that, whatever happened, Mr. and Mrs. Fletcher would see no ghosts.

Fletcher secured a curious-looking trap, and met us at the little wayside station. It was good to see his pleasure at beholding us again. The journey was so long that the short winter's day was already fading out of the sky, and it was in pitch darkness that we reached our new abode after a long, chilly drive.

Mrs. Fletcher welcomed us with a broad smile of satisfaction which was a full assurance that nothing had happened to disturb her tranquillity; and the well-spread tea-table looked very cosy and "homey," with our own silver and linen, in the low-ceiled dining-room.

The house was just to my taste—the rooms were not large, and many of them were of odd shapes. Most of the furniture was of the time of Queen Anne, with additions of queer, foreign-looking things whose age I could only guess at. The walls were thick, the window-seats deep, the passages dark. It was old enough, but, I thought, too comfortable to be ghostly.

I never believed in ghosts. It was a subject I avoided, ever since a curious illusion that once came to me during my married life—but that is another story. I had a feeling always after that as if, should I once believe in ghosts, I should begin to see them. I sometimes felt as if I had a curious inner eye which I could keep shut; and I determined not to open it while I was at Dennismore.

Darley was the only person to whom I told my former curious experience. She called it second-sight, saying it was the fruit of my mother's Highland blood. Since those days I have heard it called the Fourth Dimension. If it is, there can be no doubt that three dimensions are the most comfortable number for mortals to possess.

Dennismore Hall was mostly built on two floors, though upstairs, under the gables, were several roomy attics, quite good enough to accommodate servants. These rooms we did not, however, occupy, Mrs. Fletcher and I having agreed that, in such a lonely part of the world, it was better that our sole male protector should be within easy reach.

Ruth and I had a charming room, opening into another, occupied by Darley and Lettice; and no sleep could have been sounder than that which we all enjoyed on the night of our arrival.

Next morning our eyes unclosed on a dazzling prospect. The grand rugged sweep of a Dorsetshire valley, pine-crowned and desolate, the rush of the stream in its stony bed, the outline of the hills which lay between us and the sea, composed a whole which made one feel how good a thing was life.

It was piercingly cold, but we had large fires everywhere, Fletcher having discovered among the outhouses a store of logs which would last us the winter through.

Out of doors we rushed when breakfast was over, and explored the garden, the old stables, the empty pigsties, the deserted fowl-yard; and then, beyond our own boundaries, following the plunging stream down to the dark, still mill-pool in the deep hollow of the combe.

The mill was to let also. Its old wheel hung motionless over the weed-grown sluice. There was a great desolation about that place which made me turn round and hurry the chicks home; I felt that I did not want to linger there.

But Dennismore itself was charming. We went all over and through the house, which indeed was of no great dimensions; and Fletcher and I planned to have some fowls and a pig, to give him employment and cheer up the place a bit. Vic, our big watch-dog, was already there. I had bestowed him upon Fletcher when our household was broken up; and Ruth and Lettice had brought the two Persian pussies, Fatima and Selim, and an excitable terrier, Larkie by name; so that we were quite a household.

The great zest of existence at first was the effort to procure food on which to sustain it. We were supplied every morning from a little farm close by with milk, eggs, and butter; every other necessary we had to go and fetch for ourselves—and, until we settled down into a comprehension of the position, we had some very funny meals, productive of keen delight to the little girls.

I felt sure that I should spend a most happy winter, with my children to teach, my new strange freedom to enjoy, and leisure to develop my taste for wood-carving, so as, if possible, to add to my income thereby. When the children were gone to bed, I sat down and wrote a very grateful letter to Sidney Locke.

It was a week after our being installed that the first curious little thing happened; and, had I had no hint from Sidney, I might not have noticed it.

I had determined, in view of the untidy nature of the work, to do my wood-carving in one of the attic rooms. There was plenty of daylight there—a quality rather lacking in the low rooms downstairs; and I had brought with me an oil stove which would warm my studio thoroughly.

On the day that Mrs. Fletcher was scrubbing and preparing this room, I met her just at the foot of the twisting oak stair that led to it.

"Please ma'am, I wouldn't let Miss Ruthie run in and out them rooms while the floors is wet, if I was you," said she.

"Miss Ruthie!" I said, staring at her. "They are both gone out for their walk with Darley."

"I think you're mistaken, ma'am," said Mrs. Fletcher respectfully; "one of 'em came up the stairs just now while I was scrubbing, and went into the next attic, and, when I called that the windows was open, went down again, hurried-like."

I paused a minute. I *knew* that the children and Darley were out; there was nobody in the house but Mrs. Fletcher and me, for Fletcher was gardening, and, besides, his step could hardly be mistaken for that of a child. But on no account must I make Mrs. Fletcher uneasy, so I said:

"Oh, perhaps they have not started yet; I will go and speak to Miss Ruthie."

And I went downstairs, pondering, to find, as I had been certain that I should, that the children were nowhere on the premises.

Next day I did not visit my studio, for we were invited to tea at the vicarage, a walk of nearly two miles.

Mr. and Mrs. Rendle asked with much interest how we liked Dennismore, and in spite of their careful reserve, I could plainly see that they were surprised at our assurances of our happiness there. I was a bit anxious as to whether they would allude to the haunting before the children; but doubtless they imagined that I myself did not know of it, and they were models of discretion. The only thing said about the former tenants was by the vicar, who remarked:

"We were all glad when the Hall changed hands, the late owners were not nice people."

I should have liked to make further inquiry, but thought it better not to do so. Instead, I invited them to tea at Dennismore. I saw them exchange glances. Mrs. Rendle accepted, but said something about the evenings being dark—the vicar's throat—and her relief was very obvious when I suggested lunch instead of tea. I had a great feeling of superiority as I walked home to our haunted house that evening! How superstitious some people were!

I dreamed that night—dreamed of the idle mill wheel, and the desolate pool, and that on the brink sat a shivering child, half-clad, who sobbed and sobbed as if his heart would break.

I started awake. The night-light flickered on the warm curtains and low ceiling, and showed me Ruthie's fat form, curled up in slumber at my side; but the pitiful sobbing continued—it was still audible—it was real. Lettice must be sobbing in her sleep, and I wondered that Darley did not awake to comfort her.

Without noise I slipped out of bed, and, going to the half-open door between our rooms, I peeped through. Both the sleepers were absolutely quiet and comfortable. I crept near enough to Lettice's little bed to hear the child's soft, even breathing and see the rounded cheek and burnished curls. Then I hastened back; and it was as I stood in the freezing night, hesitating, that the idea first occurred to me that the noise I heard might be ghostly. It still went on: there is no sound so torturing to the ears of a mother as that of a child's hopeless misery. My flesh creeps now as I think of that pitiful, broken wailing. It sounded muffled, as though it came from another room—overhead, I took it to be.

Snatching a warm dressing-gown, I lit a candle, and cautiously opened the door of my room. The long, narrow passage lay in gloom outside. I listened; all sound had entirely ceased. After a few moments' waiting the silence got upon my nerves, and, drawing back into the bedroom, I closed the door.

No sobbing was now to be heard. Everything was as still, as comforting, as homelike as it could be. Then, drawing back the blind, I peered out into the night. It was pitch dark. With a glance at sleeping Ruth, I softly opened the casement and held out a candle so as to illumine the garden beds just under my window. The night was so still that the candle burned steadily. There were no large shrubs there, and, had any child been outside, the light must have attracted its attention. But there was no movement, stir, or sound. Either the sobbing was a persistent nightmare going on after having awakened me, or it was something outside the range of one's ordinary experiences. I crept back to bed, feeling very cowardly and small; next morning I patrolled the whole house and grounds without finding anything that could throw light upon the mystery.

To no one did I speak of it; I was more than willing to think it a delusion. It seemed natural that I should be nervous and unstrung just now—feeling the reaction after years of strain; a determination awoke to give no encouragement to that state of mind in which one looks searchingly into dark corners, and starts at an unexpected sound.

Next day was really lovely, and the children danced delightedly off with Fletcher to see how much ice was on the pond—a morning's uninterrupted wood-carving seemed really possible. I did just, as I passed Mrs. Fletcher on the stairs, ask her if she slept well, and she replied that, as usual, neither she nor her husband had stirred all night.

My studio was charming. It was sunny, and the stove warmed it to perfection. Work no doubt was the thing to cure morbid delusions, and for two hours I was most diligent. I had just begun to feel hungry after two hours' unbroken energy, when I heard a light footstep pattering up the uncarpeted oak stairs.

Never for a moment did such a thing seem surprising. It was the footfall of a child, doubtless Ruth or Lettice come to say that lunch awaited me. The door was fastened; it was a commonly finished garret door, with a latch which was visible on the inside. As I looked I saw the latch rise, the door slowly open, and a little boy peer round into the room. He looked about ten or eleven years old; his face was white, his dark eyes big and hollow. He was so thin that my heart ached to behold him; and his poor little hand, which grasped the woodwork of the door, was covered with sores, such as disfigure the ill-nourished children of the very poor. There was a purple bruise upon his left cheekbone. Here, doubtless, was the creature who had sobbed in the night—and I, superstitious fool, because of a foolish ghost-story, had believed his pitiful crying a delusion! I sprang up.

"Oh, poor little man!" I cried, "what do you want?"

He drew back behind the door—only his head and part of his body had been visible. As he disappeared I saw to my bewilderment that the latch was not undone, but firmly fastened. It was the work of a moment to unfasten it and look out; nobody was there.

I took a swift survey right and left. The stairhead was opposite, about twelve feet to my right. The straight passage had three other doors—all were fastened. I was not afraid of a child in broad daylight, but it seemed that he must be hidden in one of these rooms among old furniture and lumber, and his eyes had looked so scared, so full of the impulse of flight, that it seemed likely he might escape me by darting out of one room while I was searching another. It seemed imperative to secure him, so I whisked down the stair, shut the door at the foot, locked it on the outside, took away the key, and rushed downstairs to the kitchen.

Darley and Mrs. Fletcher were both there.

"Mrs. Fletcher," I gasped breathlessly, "somehow or other a child has got into this house—a little boy, who seems to be half wild with fright. He is hidden some-where in the garrets, and he must be starving! You know you heard him moving about the day before yesterday, and I woke in the night and heard him sobbing. He came and peeped at me just now, but when I spoke he ran away."

Both the servants faced me blankly.

"I think you must be mistaken, ma'am," said Darley.

"My dear Darley, I tell you I saw him; but he ran away! I have locked the door at the foot of the stairs, so he is trapped up there; will you two come and help me find him?"

They both came at once. Mrs. Fletcher remained at the stairhead to intercept him, should he run out. But the odd thing was, the rooms, all but the studio, were locked, with the keys outside. We went through them all, nevertheless.

There was no trace of a child, or of any living thing.

"It is perfectly dreadful; he must have some hiding-place," I urged. "Why does he not come out? Why is he so frightened? I spoke so gently to him."

Darley did not answer; her eyes were fixed on me with a troubled gaze, and I stopped short. I knew in my heart that the door of my studio had never really opened; all this must be mere fancy. The only person who had been told the foolish tale of haunting was the only one to be disturbed. Ah! but what of the footsteps that Mrs. Fletcher had heard upon these same oak stairs?

I began to feel a distinct lessening of my sense of gratitude to Sidney Locke.

It was difficult to know what line to adopt with the servants. Gazing at their grave, attentive faces, I realised how inconvenient, how almost impossible it would be to leave this shelter, offered me in my necessity. But if the Fletchers got unsettled, and declined to stay, what should I do? In some mysterious manner, the impression had been conveyed, by what the vicar's wife did *not* say, that no native of the neighbourhood would take service at Dennismore.

It seemed that the haunting of the house was confined to the top floor. To leave this unused was simple enough. I wished that I had kept my experience to myself; but it had seemed so idiotic to imagine that the child could be unreal!

I began to stammer out excuses; it was nightmare, overwrought nerves, a vivid fancy: I would certainly adopt Darley's advice—take a glass of wine with my dinner, and lie down.

The rest of the day was not comfortable; shaken nerves will not quiet down in a moment, such a shock leaves the victim shaky and queer. But by next morning a profound sleep had refreshed me, and I could begin to feel ashamed of myself; it is much easier to believe oneself nervous and fanciful, than that the curtain between the seen and unseen has been lifted for a moment.

All these laudable convictions were strengthened when a week passed without anything to disturb our tranquility. The children were well, and air fine, and Darley began to lose her habit of regarding me as though in apprehension of some dislocation of my mental balance.

But one night—the eighth or ninth after the first sounds, I was again awakened by the sobbing. It was too unbearable; some assurance that the thing was only fancy seemed imperatively needed. Hastening into Darley's room, I awoke her, and in a whisper bade her get up and come into my room.

Now we should see if I were mad. "Do you hear that?" I whispered.

She grew perceptibly paler; she did not need to speak; evidently she heard it too.

"Darley," I solemnly said, "dare you come up to the garrets with me, and see that there is nobody there?"

"Yes, ma'am, I dare," she answered simply. "There *is* a child up there, no doubt, as you said."

My laugh was rather mocking.

"Has he been there nine days without food? He was starving when I saw him! No, Darley, I am going to tell you the truth. This house is haunted. Mr. Locke knew that it was said to be, but he did not believe it. However, it is true, as you hear."

The dreadful sounds died away. Darley turned to me with resolution.

"It is but childish to talk so, ma'am. We know there's no such things as ghostis. But somebody's been ill-treating a child and turned his brain, and we ought to have the law of 'em. Come, ma'am, let us lock the children in here, and you come up with me to the garrets. We *must* find him."

Resolution was in her eye as she lighted two candles in glass chimneys, and softly we crept from the room and went along the passage. On the other side of it were doors of rooms which we did not use—two bedrooms, one with an adjoining dressing-room, also the bathroom.

These lay at right angles to the rooms we occupied, the passage making a sharp bend. As we turned the corner, emerging into that part which led straight to the oak stair, I stopped short.

At the door of the dressing-room there stood a man. His attitude was of one listening; in his right hand, which hung at his side, he held a cane. His face

I clearly saw, and can only say that it was one of the worst, the most degraded, the vilest, I have ever encountered. His age might be between fifty and sixty, and in my heart there rose up against him, as I gazed, a loathing which sickened me.

"Look," I whispered to Darley, "quick! What do you see—there by the door?"

She looked blank; it was plain in an instant that she saw nothing. And so it was clear that the house *was* haunted, and that I was one possessed of that much-to-be-dreaded gift, the power to see what others cannot.

"We may go back to our beds, Darley," I cried defiantly. "There is no child upstairs, any more than there is really a man there, by the door, where I see him."

Even as the words escaped me, the horror had faded and was gone; and it seems that it was all that Darley could do to drag my collapsed limbs back to bed.

The next day I wrote to Sidney Locke:

"Had you some grudge against me in the past, that you should wish to expose me to the horrors of residence in this place? If so, you have accomplished your purpose; I have suffered.

"The house is indeed haunted—haunted, as I believe, by a murderer and his victim. Fortunately I am the one who is most disturbed, but I dare not think for how long I could stand the strain; and there is, besides, to be considered the possibility that, in spite of all my care, the children may get a shock which would impair their nervous system for all the future. I am at my wits' end. Do you think the Society for Psychical Research could do anything? It is awful to contemplate a move just now, but I cannot bear this for long."

Two days after the despatch of this letter, Sidney Locke himself drove up to the door of Dennismore!

We were at tea when he arrived, and, before the little girls, nothing could of course be said respecting the object of his visit. But in every look of his I could read what he would say, his mingled anxiety and incredulity—and some other, warmer feeling, whose very existence I had in old times never suspected, and which it was surely only vanity to imagine now!

"Ten layers of birthdays on a woman's head!"

But it was certainly pleasant to see him, and the very knowledge of his solicitude brought reassurance with it.

Of course he had come to stay. There was no other place in the neighbourhood in which he could conceivably put up. So Darley prepared a room for him, and when Ruth and Lettice had gone to bed he and I sat over the fire, and I told him exactly what I had seen and heard. He seemed so staggered and upset that I was quite surprised.

"But who told you anything about the Haggards?" he said at last.

"Who are the Haggards?" I instantly rejoined.

"The people who lived in this house before my uncle bought it."

"I never heard of them," I replied, "not even their names."

"Is that really so? Have you made no inquiries in the neighbourhood?"

"None whatever. The only person who has ever spoken to us of the house at all has been the vicar, who said that the late owners were not nice people, and that he was glad when the place changed hands."

"Well," he said, after a considerable pause of surprise, "the house belonged to a naval captain named Newman. Haggard was his brother-in-law, a man who had never done any good, but for the sake of his sister, who was married to the brute, Newman allowed them to live here, and gave them the care of his only boy, whose mother was dead. Haggard seems to have thought that, as the captain's life was precarious, it would be a good thing to rid himself of the boy, and get the house left to him, and the money too. His wife must have been pretty nearly as bad as he, or else completely terrorised. Their story was that the child was half-witted, stubborn, and disgusting in his habits. But, remote though the place is, whispers of their cruelty got abroad. At last the child disappeared, and they gave out that he had run away to sea, which they declared he had often threatened to do. The father's frantic grief and indignation had exactly the contrary effect to that which Haggard intended. He turned them both out, sold the place, and made a will leaving his money to the Society for Befriending Waifs and Strays. He is still alive, and so are the Haggards, for aught I know to the contrary."

"The child was murdered," I said with conviction; "and his bones lie hid somewhere about this house or grounds, I feel certain."

"It seems to me probable that you are right," he said, after more thought. "Of course, it was likely that a child ill-treated might run away, but still more likely that the man should get rid of him, if he thought he could do so with impunity."

"He hadn't the spirit to run away," I said with a shudder. "A more down-trodden, desolate creature you never saw."

"But ghost-stories," he presently added with a puzzled air, "are not true."

"I can't say," I replied. "I can only truly tell you what I have seen and heard, and also that Mrs. Fletcher heard steps, and Darley heard sobbing. I am not afraid, though—that is, not now that you are here."

He caught me up quickly.

"Not now that I am here," he began, and stopped. "I know," he said, "that you believe I never meant to expose you to anything of the sort."

"Of course I know it, and I am ashamed to have written to you as I did; but I was overwrought, and it did seem as though I was never to have any peace. Besides," I added, somewhat irrelevantly, "I hadn't seen you then."

"Ah! And now that you have seen me, you are inclined to believe me honest?"

"Yes."

"And trustworthy?"

"Yes."

"Well, I'll try to live up to that opinion," he replied, jumping up suddenly and walking about the room. "Then may I stay here, say a week, and continue investigations?"

I agreed, and, as it was growing late, we separated.

Next day there was no question of investigating, nor of anything else but skating.

The mill-pond was five inches thick in glossy black ice, and Ruth and Lettice whirled us off directly after breakfast. They were like mad things with pleasure when they found that Sidney could cut figures; as for me, I could not, however I strove, shake off from my mind the sinister impression which that place always made upon me.

I could not be gay there; the house had never impressed me in the same way. But the pool! If ever a place appealed to me directly as being haunted, it was that water. The hush, the curious stillness, the black depths of wintry firs and larches that kept the sun from it all day long—the sullen aspect of the torpid wheel, hanging as though in horror of what it knew lay under the smooth surface—it all wrought upon my nerves till I longed to fly the spot. And yet I did not like to leave the care of the children to Sidney, and I could not plead my fantastic fears.

We went home to dinner, and then I found, to my unspeakable woe, that it was necessary for me to face the awful place again. Lettice was just beginning to grasp the true science of the outside edge, and Sidney really seemed quite as keen as she was herself about it.

Back we all went, and I glided to and fro, trying hard to think of other things, to forget how I hated the wicked atmosphere that overhung me.

The short afternoon began to close in; the children must not be out in the dusk. I issued the order to return, and, amid much grumbling, they sat down on the bank for Sidney to take off their skates.

I came slowly skating down the pond to join them; and some strange impulse drew my eyes to the opposite bank, where the dense shadow of the thick trees loomed blackest.

There lay something on the surface of the pool, but it looked half submerged, as though it floated. Slowly, slowly I drew nearer, with the fascination of horror; it was the body of a child!

I saw the small chin flung helplessly back, the grey outline of the pinched face, the sodden limpness of the impotent limbs.

Did they not see it too?... I held my breath in utter dread. It may have been thirty seconds, it seemed to me that hours elapsed, that ages of awful possibilities rolled over my head, before I began to realise that the ice was five inches thick, and that a floating corpse must be an illusion of the filmiest kind.

Through the roaring in my ears I heard the high-pitched, laughing voices of the children borne on the frozen twilight air; an oppression gripped me—a feeling of deadly nausea; the smoky redness of the west was a blur of blood and fire to my dazzled eyes.

I did not say anything, so they tell me. I stood as still as if the ice had reached my heart. They became suddenly aware of something odd or unusual in my rigidity. Sidney crossed the pond in a few strokes; his coming was inaudible to me, but he was in time to catch me as I fell in a fainting-fit which lasted for more than two hours.

In the morning I had developed feverish symptoms, and for several days I was ill with what the doctor called a chill, with a good deal of fever and consequent delirium.

During that delirium the apparition of the little boy went and came continually. He stood by my bed, he tapped at my door, he crouched on my hearth as if for warmth. To such a phantom I attach, of course, no importance whatever; it was the direct result of temperature, and vanished completely as soon as the clinical thermometer could be induced to register less than a hundred.

I have never seen it since; and you may consequently be tempted to think, as most people do who hear this story, that the whole of the haunting of Dennismore Hall was merely febrile in its character—the result of my constitution having been in a state of working up for a pretty sharp attack of illness.

As to the justice of such a view, you who have heard the facts must judge for yourselves; but to what I have already related please add the following before arriving at a conclusion:

When the thaw came the mill-pond was dragged, and the bones of a child were found in the slime just beneath the scene of my vision.

No means of identification were forthcoming, beyond the fact that the skeleton was that of a boy, and of the age of Captain Newman's son at the time of his disappearance.

Whether the miserable little one really was murdered, or threw himself into the water, or met his death by accident will never be known. His father had his bones duly laid in the churchyard beside those of the mother whose early death had left him so pitifully an orphan. The Haggards were brought to trial, but though there was plenty of evidence of cruelty and miserliness forthcoming, there was nothing to convict of murder. The last I heard of them was that they were in the workhouse, so they are expiating their crime at least in part.

We still live at Dennismore part of the year, and have no difficulty in letting it when we are not there ourselves. It is not in the least haunted—at least, as the tradesmen say, there have been "no complaints."

And since the vicar laid those pathetic little bones to "rest beneath the clever sod," with the trumpet notes of S. Paul's anthem of the Resurrection, neither he nor his wife are any longer nervous about coming to tea with us, even in the dusk of a winter's evening.

THE LOST GHOST*

Mary E. Wilkins

Mrs. John Emerson, sitting with her needlework beside the window, looked out and saw Mrs. Rhoda Meserve coming down the street, and knew at once by the trend of her steps and the cant of her head that she meditated turning in at her gate. She also knew by a certain something about her general carriage—a thrusting forward of the neck, a bustling hitch of the shoulders—that she had important news. Rhoda Meserve always had the news as soon as the news was in being, and generally Mrs. John Emerson was the first to whom she imparted it. The two women had been friends ever since Mrs. Meserve had married Simon Meserve and come to the village to live.

Mrs. Meserve was a pretty woman, moving with graceful flirts of ruffling skirts; her clear-cut, nervous face, as delicately tinted as a shell, looked brightly from the plumy brim of a black hat at Mrs. Emerson in the window. Mrs. Emerson was glad to see her coming. She returned the greeting with enthusiasm, then rose hurriedly, ran into the cold parlour and brought out one of the best rocking-chairs. She was just in time, after drawing it up beside the opposite window, to greet her friend at the door.

"Good-afternoon," said she. "I declare, I'm real glad to see you. I've been alone all day. John went to the city this morning. I thought of coming over to your house this afternoon, but I couldn't bring my sewing very well. I am putting the ruffles on my new black dress skirt."

"Well, I didn't have a thing on hand except my crochet work," responded Mrs. Meserve, "and I thought I'd just run over a few minutes."

"I'm real glad you did," repeated Mrs. Emerson. "Take your things right off. Here, I'll put them on my bed in the bedroom. Take the rocking-chair."

Mrs. Meserve settled herself in the parlour rocking-chair, while Mrs. Emerson

---

* "The Lost Ghost" appeared in Wilkins's collection *The Wind in the Rose-bush and Other Stories of the Supernatural* (New York: Doubleday, Page, 1903). The current text is based on this edition. Obvious typographical errors and inconsistencies have been silently corrected.

carried her shawl and hat into the little adjoining bedroom. When she returned
Mrs. Meserve was rocking peacefully and was already at work hooking blue wool
in and out.

"That's real pretty," said Mrs. Emerson.

"Yes, I think it's pretty," replied Mrs. Meserve.

"I suppose it's for the church fair?"

"Yes. I don't suppose it'll bring enough to pay for the worsted, let alone the
work, but I suppose I've got to make something."

"How much did that one you made for the fair last year bring?"

"Twenty-five cents."

"It's wicked, ain't it?"

"I rather guess it is. It takes me a week every minute I can get to make one. I
wish those that bought such things for twenty-five cents had to make them. Guess
they'd sing another song. Well, I suppose I oughtn't to complain as long as it is
for the Lord, but sometimes it does seem as if the Lord didn't get much out of it."

"Well, it's pretty work," said Mrs. Emerson, sitting down at the opposite window and taking up her dress skirt.

"Yes, it is real pretty work. I just *love* to crochet."

The two women rocked and sewed and crocheted in silence for two or three
minutes. They were both waiting. Mrs. Meserve waited for the other's curiosity to
develop in order that her news might have, as it were, a befitting stage entrance.
Mrs. Emerson waited for the news. Finally she could wait no longer.

"Well, what's the news?" said she.

"Well, I don't know as there's anything very particular," hedged the other
woman, prolonging the situation.

"Yes, there is; you can't cheat me," replied Mrs. Emerson.

"Now, how do you know?"

"By the way you look."

Mrs. Meserve laughed consciously and rather vainly.

"Well, Simon says my face is so expressive I can't hide anything more than
five minutes no matter how hard I try," said she. "Well, there is some news. Simon
came home with it this noon. He heard it in South Dayton. He had some business
over there this morning. The old Sargent place is let."

Mrs. Emerson dropped her sewing and stared.

"You don't say so!"

"Yes, it is."

"Who to?"

"Why, some folks from Boston that moved to South Dayton last year. They haven't been satisfied with the house they had there—it wasn't large enough. The man has got considerable property and can afford to live pretty well. He's got a wife and his unmarried sister in the family. The sister's got money, too. He does business in Boston and it's just as easy to get to Boston from here as from South Dayton, and so they're coming here. You know the old Sargent house is a splendid place."

"Yes, it's the handsomest house in town, but——"

"Oh, Simon said they told him about that and he just laughed. Said he wasn't afraid and neither was his wife and sister. Said he'd risk ghosts rather than little tucked-up sleeping-rooms without any sun, like they've had in the Dayton house. Said he'd rather risk *seeing* ghosts, than risk being ghosts themselves. Simon said they said he was a great hand to joke."

"Oh, well," said Mrs. Emerson, "it is a beautiful house, and maybe there isn't anything in those stories. It never seemed to me they came very straight anyway. I never took much stock in them. All I thought was—if his wife was nervous."

"Nothing in creation would hire me to go into a house that I'd ever heard a word against of that kind," declared Mrs. Meserve with emphasis. "I wouldn't go into that house if they would give me the rent. I've seen enough of haunted houses to last me as long as I live."

Mrs. Emerson's face acquired the expression of a hunting hound.

"Have you?" she asked in an intense whisper.

"Yes, I have. I don't want any more of it."

"Before you came here?"

"Yes; before I was married—when I was quite a girl."

Mrs. Meserve had not married young. Mrs. Emerson had mental calculations when she heard that.

"Did you really live in a house that was——" she whispered fearfully.

Mrs. Meserve nodded solemnly.

"Did you really ever—see—anything——"

Mrs. Meserve nodded.

"You didn't see anything that did you any harm?"

"No, I didn't see anything that did me harm looking at it in one way, but it don't do anybody in this world any good to see things that haven't any business to be seen in it. You never get over it."

There was a moment's silence. Mrs. Emerson's features seemed to sharpen.

"Well, of course I don't want to urge you," said she, "if you don't feel like talking about it; but maybe it might do you good to tell it out, if it's on your mind, worrying you."

"I try to put it out of my mind," said Mrs. Meserve.

"Well, it's just as you feel."

"I never told anybody but Simon," said Mrs. Meserve. "I never felt as if it was wise perhaps. I didn't know what folks might think. So many don't believe in anything they can't understand, that they might think my mind wasn't right. Simon advised me not to talk about it. He said he didn't believe it was anything supernatural, but he had to own up that he couldn't give any explanation for it to save his life. He had to own up that he didn't believe anybody could. Then he said he wouldn't talk about it. He said lots of folks would sooner tell folks my head wasn't right than to own up they couldn't see through it."

"I'm sure I wouldn't say so," returned Mrs. Emerson reproachfully. "You know better than that, I hope."

"Yes, I do," replied Mrs. Meserve. "I know you wouldn't say so."

"And I wouldn't tell it to a soul if you didn't want me to."

"Well, I'd rather you wouldn't."

"I won't speak of it even to Mr. Emerson."

"I'd rather you wouldn't even to him."

"I won't."

Mrs. Emerson took up her dress skirt again; Mrs. Meserve hooked up another loop of blue wool. Then she begun:

"Of course," said she, "I ain't going to say positively that I believe or disbelieve in ghosts, but all I tell you is what I saw. I can't explain it. I don't pretend I can, for I can't. If you can, well and good; I shall be glad, for it will stop tormenting me as it has done and always will otherwise. There hasn't been a day nor a night since it happened that I haven't thought of it, and always I have felt the shivers go down my back when I did."

"That's an awful feeling," Mrs. Emerson said.

"Ain't it? Well, it happened before I was married, when I was a girl and lived in East Wilmington. It was the first year I lived there. You know my family all died five years before that. I told you."

Mrs. Emerson nodded.

"Well, I went there to teach school, and I went to board with a Mrs. Amelia Dennison and her sister, Mrs. Bird. Abby, her name was—Abby Bird. She was a widow; she had never had any children. She had a little money—Mrs. Dennison didn't have any—and she had come to East Wilmington and bought the house they lived in. It was a real pretty house, though it was very old and run down. It had cost Mrs. Bird a good deal to put it in order. I guess that was the reason they took me to board. I guess they thought it would help along a little. I guess what I paid for my board about kept us all in victuals. Mrs. Bird had enough to live on if they were careful, but she had spent so much fixing up the old house that they must have been a little pinched for awhile.

"Anyhow, they took me to board, and I thought I was pretty lucky to get in there. I had a nice room, big and sunny and furnished pretty, the paper and paint all new, and everything as neat as wax. Mrs. Dennison was one of the best cooks I ever saw, and I had a little stove in my room, and there was always a nice fire there when I got home from school. I thought I hadn't been in such a nice place since I lost my own home, until I had been there about three weeks.

"I had been there about three weeks before I found it out, though I guess it had been going on ever since they had been in the house, and that was most four months. They hadn't said anything about it, and I didn't wonder, for there they had just bought the house and been to so much expense and trouble fixing it up.

"Well, I went there in September. I begun my school the first Monday. I remember it was a real cold fall, there was a frost the middle of September, and I had to put on my winter coat. I remember when I came home that night (let me see, I began school on a Monday, and that was two weeks from the next Thursday), I took off my coat downstairs and laid it on the table in the front entry. It was a real nice coat—heavy black broadcloth trimmed with fur; I had had it the winter before. Mrs. Bird called after me as I went upstairs that I ought not to leave it in the front entry for fear somebody might come in and take it, but I only laughed and called back to her that I wasn't afraid. I never was much afraid of burglars.

"Well, though it was hardly the middle of September, it was a real cold night. I remember my room faced west, and the sun was getting low, and the sky was a pale yellow and purple, just as you see it sometimes in the winter when there is going to be a cold snap. I rather think that was the night the frost came the first time. I know Mrs. Dennison covered up some flowers she had in the front yard, anyhow. I remember looking out and seeing an old green plaid shawl of hers over the verbena bed. There was a fire in my little wood-stove. Mrs. Bird made it, I know. She was a real motherly sort of woman; she always seemed to be the happiest when she was doing something to make other folks happy and comfortable. Mrs. Dennison told me she had always been so. She said she had coddled her husband within an inch of his life. 'It's lucky Abby never had any children,' she said, 'for she would have spoilt them.'

"Well, that night I sat down beside my nice little fire and ate an apple. There was a plate of nice apples on my table. Mrs. Bird put them there. I was always very fond of apples. Well, I sat down and ate an apple, and was having a beautiful time, and thinking how lucky I was to have got board in such a place with such nice folks, when I heard a queer little sound at my door. It was such a little hesitating sort of sound that it sounded more like a fumble than a knock, as if someone very timid, with very little hands, was feeling along the door, not quite daring to knock. For a minute I thought it was a mouse. But I waited and it came again, and then I made up my mind it was a knock, but a very little scared one, so I said, 'Come in.'

"But nobody came in, and then presently I heard the knock again. Then I got up and opened the door, thinking it was very queer, and I had a frightened feeling without knowing why.

"Well, I opened the door, and the first thing I noticed was a draught of cold air, as if the front door downstairs was open, but there was a strange close smell about the cold draught. It smelled more like a cellar that had been shut up for years, than out-of-doors. Then I saw something. I saw my coat first. The thing that held it was so small that I couldn't see much of anything else. Then I saw a little white face with eyes so scared and wishful that they seemed as if they might eat a hole in anybody's heart. It was a dreadful little face, with something about it which made it different from any other face on earth, but it was so pitiful that somehow it did away a good deal with the dreadfulness. And there were two little hands spotted purple with the cold, holding up my winter coat, and a strange little far-away voice said: 'I can't find my mother.'

"'For Heaven's sake,' I said, 'who are you?'

"Then the little voice said again: 'I can't find my mother.'

"All the time I could smell the cold and I saw that it was about the child; that cold was clinging to her as if she had come out of some deadly cold place. Well, I took my coat, I did not know what else to do, and the cold was clinging to that. It was as cold as if it had come off ice. When I had the coat I could see the child more plainly. She was dressed in one little white garment made very simply. It was a nightgown, only very long, quite covering her feet, and I could see dimly through it her little thin body mottled purple with the cold. Her face did not look so cold; that was a clear waxen white. Her hair was dark, but it looked as if it might be dark only because it was so damp, almost wet, and might really be light hair. It clung very close to her forehead, which was round and white. She would have been very beautiful if she had not been so dreadful.

"'Who are you?' says I again, looking at her.

"She looked at me with her terrible pleading eyes and did not say anything.

"'What are you?' says I. Then she went away. She did not seem to run or walk like other children. She flitted, like one of those little filmy white butterflies, that don't seem like real ones they are so light, and move as if they had no weight. But she looked back from the head of the stairs. 'I can't find my mother,' said she, and I never heard such a voice.

"'Who is your mother?' says I, but she was gone.

"Well, I thought for a moment I should faint away. The room got dark and I heard a singing in my ears. Then I flung my coat onto the bed. My hands were as cold as ice from holding it, and I stood in my door, and called first Mrs. Bird and then Mrs. Dennison. I didn't dare go down over the stairs where that had gone. It seemed to me I should go mad if I didn't see somebody or something like other folks on the face of the earth. I thought I should never make anybody hear, but I could hear them stepping about downstairs, and I could smell biscuits baking for supper. Somehow the smell of those biscuits seemed the only natural thing left to keep me in my right mind. I didn't dare go over those stairs. I just stood there and called, and finally I heard the entry door open and Mrs. Bird called back:

"'What is it? Did you call, Miss Arms?'

"'Come up here; come up here as quick as you can, both of you,' I screamed out; 'quick, quick, quick!'

"I heard Mrs. Bird tell Mrs. Dennison: 'Come quick, Amelia, something is the matter in Miss Arms' room.' It struck me even then that she expressed herself rather queerly, and it struck me as very queer, indeed, when they both got upstairs and I saw that they knew what had happened, or that they knew of what nature the happening was.

"'What is it, dear?' asked Mrs. Bird, and her pretty, loving voice had a strained sound. I saw her look at Mrs. Dennison and I saw Mrs. Dennison look back at her.

"'For God's sake,' says I, and I never spoke so before—'for God's sake, what was it brought my coat upstairs?'

"'What was it like?' asked Mrs. Dennison in a sort of failing voice, and she looked at her sister again and her sister looked back at her.

"'It was a child I have never seen here before. It looked like a child,' says I, 'but I never saw a child so dreadful, and it had on a nightgown, and said she couldn't find her mother. Who was it? What was it?'

"I thought for a minute Mrs. Dennison was going to faint, but Mrs. Bird hung onto her and rubbed her hands, and whispered in her ear (she had the cooingest kind of voice), and I ran and got her a glass of cold water. I tell you it took considerable courage to go downstairs alone, but they had set a lamp on the entry table so I could see. I don't believe I could have spunked up enough to have gone downstairs in the dark, thinking every second that child might be close to me. The lamp and the smell of the biscuits baking seemed to sort of keep my courage up, but I tell you I didn't waste much time going down those stairs and out into the kitchen for a glass of water. I pumped as if the house was afire, and I grabbed the first thing I came across in the shape of a tumbler: it was a painted one that Mrs. Dennison's Sunday school class gave her, and it was meant for a flower vase.

"Well, I filled it and then ran upstairs. I felt every minute as if something would catch my feet, and I held the glass to Mrs. Dennison's lips, while Mrs. Bird held her head up, and she took a good long swallow, then she looked hard at the tumbler.

"'Yes,' says I, 'I know I got this one, but I took the first I came across, and it isn't hurt a mite.'

"'Don't get the painted flowers wet,' says Mrs. Dennison very feebly, 'they'll wash off if you do.'

"'I'll be real careful,' says I. I knew she set a sight by that painted tumbler.

"The water seemed to do Mrs. Dennison good, for presently she pushed Mrs. Bird away and sat up. She had been laying down on my bed.

"'I'm all over it now,' says she, but she was terribly white, and her eyes looked as if they saw something outside things. Mrs. Bird wasn't much better, but she always had a sort of settled sweet, good look that nothing could disturb to any great extent. I knew I looked dreadful, for I caught a glimpse of myself in the glass, and I would hardly have known who it was.

"Mrs. Dennison, she slid off the bed and walked sort of tottery to a chair. 'I was silly to give way so,' says she.

"'No, you wasn't silly, sister,' says Mrs. Bird. 'I don't know what this means any more than you do, but whatever it is, no one ought to be called silly for being overcome by anything so different from other things which we have known all our lives.'

"Mrs. Dennison looked at her sister, then she looked at me, then back at her sister again, and Mrs. Bird spoke as if she had been asked a question.

"'Yes,' says she, 'I do think Miss Arms ought to be told—that is, I think she ought to be told all we know ourselves.'

"'That isn't much,' said Mrs. Dennison with a dying-away sort of sigh. She looked as if she might faint away again any minute. She was a real delicate-looking woman, but it turned out she was a good deal stronger than poor Mrs. Bird.

"'No, there isn't much we do know,' says Mrs. Bird, 'but what little there is she ought to know. I felt as if she ought to when she first came here.'

"'Well, I didn't feel quite right about it,' said Mrs. Dennison, 'but I kept hoping it might stop, and any way, that it might never trouble her, and you had put so much in the house, and we needed the money, and I didn't know but she might be nervous and think she couldn't come, and I didn't want to take a man boarder.'

"'And aside from the money, we were very anxious to have you come, my dear,' says Mrs. Bird.

"'Yes,' says Mrs. Dennison, 'we wanted the young company in the house; we were lonesome, and we both of us took a great liking to you the minute we set eyes on you.'

"And I guess they meant what they said, both of them. They were beautiful women, and nobody could be any kinder to me than they were, and I never blamed them for not telling me before, and, as they said, there wasn't really much to tell.

"They hadn't any sooner fairly bought the house, and moved into it, than they began to see and hear things. Mrs. Bird said they were sitting together in the sitting-room one evening when they heard it the first time. She said her sister was knitting lace (Mrs. Dennison made beautiful knitted lace) and she was reading the *Missionary Herald* (Mrs. Bird was very much interested in mission work), when all of a sudden they heard something. She heard it first and she laid down her *Missionary Herald* and listened, and then Mrs. Dennison she saw her listening and she drops her lace. 'What is it you are listening to, Abby?' says she. Then it came again and they both heard, and the cold shivers went down their backs to hear it, though they didn't know why. 'It's the cat, isn't it?' says Mrs. Bird.

"'It isn't any cat,' says Mrs. Dennison.

"'Oh, I guess it *must* be the cat; maybe he's got a mouse,' says Mrs. Bird, real cheerful, to calm down Mrs. Dennison, for she saw she was 'most scared to death, and she was always afraid of her fainting away. Then she opens the door and calls, 'Kitty, kitty, kitty!' They had brought their cat with them in a basket when they came to East Wilmington to live. It was a real handsome tiger cat, a tommy, and he knew a lot.

"Well, she called 'Kitty, kitty, kitty!' and sure enough the kitty came, and when he came in the door he gave a big yawl that didn't sound unlike what they had heard.

"'There, sister, here he is; you see it was the cat,' says Mrs. Bird. 'Poor kitty!'

"But Mrs. Dennison she eyed the cat, and she give a great screech.

"'What's that? What's that?' says she.

"'What's what?' says Mrs. Bird, pretending to herself that she didn't see what her sister meant.

"'Somethin's got hold of that cat's tail,' says Mrs. Dennison. 'Somethin's got hold of his tail. It's pulled straight out, an' he can't get away. Just hear him yawl!'

"'It isn't anything,' says Mrs. Bird, but even as she said that she could see a little hand holding fast to that cat's tail, and then the child seemed to sort of clear out of the dimness behind the hand, and the child was sort of laughing then, instead of looking sad, and she said that was a great deal worse. She said that laugh was the most awful and the saddest thing she ever heard.

"Well, she was so dumfounded that she didn't know what to do, and she couldn't sense at first that it was anything supernatural. She thought it must be one of the neighbour's children who had run away and was making free of their house, and was teasing their cat, and that they must be just nervous to feel so upset by it. So she speaks up sort of sharp.

"'Don't you know that you mustn't pull the kitty's tail?' says she. 'Don't you know you hurt the poor kitty, and he'll scratch you if you don't take care. Poor kitty, you mustn't hurt him.'

"And with that she said the child stopped pulling that cat's tail and went to stroking him just as soft and pitiful, and the cat put his back up and rubbed and purred as if he liked it. The cat never seemed a mite afraid, and that seemed queer, for I had always heard that animals were dreadfully afraid of ghosts; but then, that was a pretty harmless little sort of ghost.

"Well, Mrs. Bird said the child stroked that cat, while she and Mrs. Dennison stood watching it, and holding onto each other, for, no matter how hard they tried to think it was all right, it didn't look right. Finally Mrs. Dennison she spoke.

"'What's your name, little girl?' says she.

"Then the child looks up and stops stroking the cat, and says she can't find her mother, just the way she said it to me. Then Mrs. Dennison she gave such a gasp that Mrs. Bird thought she was going to faint away, but she didn't. 'Well, who is your mother?' says she. But the child just says again 'I can't find my mother—I can't find my mother.'

"'Where do you live, dear?' says Mrs. Bird.

"'I can't find my mother,' says the child.

"Well, that was the way it was. Nothing happened. Those two women stood there hanging onto each other, and the child stood in front of them, and they asked her questions, and everything she would say was: 'I can't find my mother.'

"Then Mrs. Bird tried to catch hold of the child, for she thought in spite of what she saw that perhaps she was nervous and it was a real child, only perhaps not quite right in its head, that had run away in her little nightgown after she had been put to bed.

"She tried to catch the child. She had an idea of putting a shawl around it and going out—she was such a little thing she could have carried her easy enough— and trying to find out to which of the neighbours she belonged. But the minute she moved toward the child there wasn't any child there; there was only that little voice seeming to come from nothing, saying 'I can't find my mother,' and presently that died away.

"Well, that same thing kept happening, or something very much the same. Once in awhile Mrs. Bird would be washing dishes, and all at once the child would be standing beside her with the dish-towel, wiping them. Of course, that was terrible. Mrs. Bird would wash the dishes all over. Sometimes she didn't tell Mrs. Dennison, it made her so nervous. Sometimes when they were making cake they would find the raisins all picked over, and sometimes little sticks of kindling-wood would be found laying beside the kitchen stove. They never knew when they would come across that child, and always she kept saying over and over that she couldn't find her mother. They never tried talking to her, except once in awhile Mrs. Bird would get desperate and ask her something, but the child never seemed to hear it; she always kept right on saying that she couldn't find her mother.

"After they had told me all they had to tell about their experience with the child, they told me about the house and the people that had lived there before they did. It seemed something dreadful had happened in that house. And the land agent had never let on to them. I don't think they would have bought it if he had, no matter how cheap it was, for even if folks aren't really afraid of anything, they don't want to live in houses where such dreadful things have happened that you keep thinking about them. I know after they told me I should never have stayed there another night, if I hadn't thought so much of them, no matter how comfortable I was made; and I never was nervous, either. But I stayed. Of course, it didn't happen in my room. If it had I could not have stayed."

"What was it?" asked Mrs. Emerson in an awed voice.

"It was an awful thing. That child had lived in the house with her father and mother two years before. They had come—or the father had—from a real good family. He had a good situation: he was a drummer for a big leather house in the city, and they lived real pretty, with plenty to do with. But the mother was a real wicked woman. She was as handsome as a picture, and they said she came from good sort of people enough in Boston, but she was bad clean through, though she was real pretty spoken and most everybody liked her. She used to dress out and make a great show, and she never seemed to take much interest in the child, and folks began to say she wasn't treated right.

"The woman had a hard time keeping a girl. For some reason one wouldn't stay. They would leave and then talk about her awfully, telling all kinds of things. People didn't believe it at first; then they began to. They said that the woman made that little thing, though she wasn't much over five years old, and small and babyish for her age, do most of the work, what there was done; they said the house used to look like a pig-sty when she didn't have help. They said the little thing used to stand on a chair and wash dishes, and they'd seen her carrying in sticks of wood most as big as she was many a time, and they'd heard her mother scolding her. The woman was a fine singer, and had a voice like a screech-owl when she scolded.

"The father was away most of the time, and when that happened he had been away out West for some weeks. There had been a married man hanging about the mother for some time, and folks had talked some; but they weren't sure there was anything wrong, and he was a man very high up, with money, so they kept pretty still for fear he would hear of it and make trouble for them, and of course nobody was sure, though folks did say afterward that the father of the child had ought to have been told.

"But that was very easy to say; it wouldn't have been so easy to find anybody who would have been willing to tell him such a thing as that, especially when they weren't any too sure. He set his eyes by his wife, too. They said all he seemed to think of was to earn money to buy things to deck her out in. And he about worshiped the child, too. They said he was a real nice man. The men that are treated so bad mostly are real nice men. I've always noticed that.

"Well, one morning that man that there had been whispers about was missing. He had been gone quite a while, though, before they really knew that he was missing, because he had gone away and told his wife that he had to go to New York on business and might be gone a week, and not to worry if he didn't get home, and not to worry if he didn't write, because he should be thinking from day to day that he might take the next train home and there would be no use in writing. So the wife waited, and she tried not to worry until it was two days over the week, then she run into a neighbour's and fainted dead away on the floor; and then they made inquiries and found out that he had skipped—with some money that didn't belong to him, too.

"Then folks began to ask where was that woman, and they found out by comparing notes that nobody had seen her since the man went away; but three or four women remembered that she had told them that she thought of taking the child and going to Boston to visit her folks, so when they hadn't seen her around, and the house shut, they jumped to the conclusion that was where she was. They were the neighbours that lived right around her, but they didn't have much to do with her, and she'd gone out of her way to tell them about her Boston plan, and they didn't make much reply when she did.

"Well, there was this house shut up, and the man and woman missing and the child. Then all of a sudden one of the women that lived the nearest remembered something. She remembered that she had waked up three nights running, thinking she heard a child crying somewhere, and once she waked up her husband, but he said it must be the Bisbees' little girl, and she thought it must be. The child wasn't well and was always crying. It used to have colic spells, especially at night. So she didn't think any more about it until this came up, then all of a sudden she did think of it. She told what she had heard, and finally folks began to think they had better enter that house and see if there was anything wrong.

"Well, they did enter it, and they found that child dead, locked in one of the rooms. (Mrs. Dennison and Mrs. Bird never used that room; it was a back bedroom on the second floor.)

"Yes, they found that poor child there, starved to death, and frozen, though they weren't sure she had frozen to death, for she was in bed with clothes enough to keep her pretty warm when she was alive. But she had been there a week, and she was nothing but skin and bone. It looked as if the mother had locked her into the house when she went away, and told her not to make any noise for fear the neighbours would hear her and find out that she herself had gone.

"Mrs. Dennison said she couldn't really believe that the woman had meant to have her own child starved to death. Probably she thought the little thing would raise somebody, or folks would try to get in the house and find her. Well, whatever she thought, there the child was, dead.

"But that wasn't all. The father came home, right in the midst of it; the child was just buried, and he was beside himself. And—he went on the track of his wife, and he found her, and he shot her dead; it was in all the papers at the time; then he disappeared. Nothing had been seen of him since. Mrs. Dennison said that she thought he had either made way with himself or got out of the country, nobody knew, but they did know there was something wrong with the house.

"'I knew folks acted queer when they asked me how I liked it when we first came here,' says Mrs. Dennison, 'but I never dreamed why till we saw the child that night.'"

"I never heard anything like it in my life," said Mrs. Emerson, staring at the other woman with awestruck eyes.

"I thought you'd say so," said Mrs. Meserve. "You don't wonder that I ain't disposed to speak light when I hear there is anything queer about a house, do you?"

"No, I don't, after that," Mrs. Emerson said.

"But that ain't all," said Mrs. Meserve.

"Did you see it again?" Mrs. Emerson asked.

"Yes, I saw it a number of times before the last time. It was lucky I wasn't nervous, or I never could have stayed there, much as I liked the place and much as I thought of those two women; they were beautiful women, and no mistake. I loved those women. I hope Mrs. Dennison will come and see me sometime.

"Well, I stayed, and I never knew when I'd see that child. I got so I was very careful to bring everything of mine upstairs, and not leave any little thing in my room that needed doing, for fear she would come lugging up my coat or hat or gloves or I'd find things done when there'd been no live being in the room to do them. I can't tell you how I dreaded seeing her; and worse than the seeing her was the hearing her say, 'I can't find my mother.' It was enough to make your blood run cold. I never heard a living child cry for its mother that was anything so pitiful as that dead one. It was enough to break your heart.

"She used to come and say that to Mrs. Bird oftener than to any one else. Once I heard Mrs. Bird say she wondered if it was possible that the poor little thing couldn't really find her mother in the other world, she had been such a wicked woman.

"But Mrs. Dennison told her she didn't think she ought to speak so nor even think so, and Mrs. Bird said she shouldn't wonder if she was right. Mrs. Bird was always very easy to put in the wrong. She was a good woman, and one that couldn't do things enough for other folks. It seemed as if that was what she lived on. I don't think she was ever so scared by that poor little ghost, as much as she pitied it, and she was 'most heartbroken because she couldn't do anything for it, as she could have done for a live child.

"'It seems to me sometimes as if I should die if I can't get that awful little white robe off that child and get her in some clothes and feed her and stop her looking for her mother,' I heard her say once, and she was in earnest. She cried when she said it. That wasn't long before she died.

"Now I am coming to the strangest part of it all. Mrs. Bird died very sudden. One morning—it was Saturday, and there wasn't any school—I went downstairs to breakfast, and Mrs. Bird wasn't there; there was nobody but Mrs. Dennison. She was pouring out the coffee when I came in. 'Why, where's Mrs. Bird?' says I.

"'Abby ain't feeling very well this morning,' says she; 'there isn't much the matter, I guess, but she didn't sleep very well, and her head aches, and she's sort of chilly, and I told her I thought she'd better stay in bed till the house gets warm.'

It was a very cold morning.

"'Maybe she's got cold,' says I.

"'Yes, I guess she has,' says Mrs. Dennison. 'I guess she's got cold. She'll be up before long. Abby ain't one to stay in bed a minute longer than she can help.'

"Well, we went on eating our breakfast, and all at once a shadow flickered across one wall of the room and over the ceiling the way a shadow will sometimes when somebody passes the window outside. Mrs. Dennison and I both looked up, then out of the window; then Mrs. Dennison she gives a scream.

"'Why, Abby's crazy!' says she. 'There she is out this bitter cold morning, and—and——' She didn't finish, but she meant the child. For we were both looking out, and we saw, as plain as we ever saw anything in our lives, Mrs. Abby Bird walking off over the white snow-path with that child holding fast to her hand, nestling close to her as if she had found her own mother.

"'She's dead,' says Mrs. Dennison, clutching hold of me hard. 'She's dead; my sister is dead!'

"She was. We hurried upstairs as fast as we could go, and she was dead in her bed, and smiling as if she was dreaming, and one arm and hand was stretched out as if something had hold of it; and it couldn't be straightened even at the last—it lay out over her casket at the funeral."

"Was the child ever seen again?" asked Mrs. Emerson in a shaking voice.

"No," replied Mrs. Meserve; "that child was never seen again after she went out of the yard with Mrs. Bird."

THE STRIDING PLACE*

Gertrude Atherton

Weigall, continental and detached, tired early of grouse-shooting. To stand propped against a sod fence while his host's workmen routed up the birds with long poles and drove them towards the waiting guns, made him feel himself a parody on the ancestors who had roamed the moors and forests of this West Riding of Yorkshire in hot pursuit of game worth the killing. But when in England in August he always accepted whatever proffered for the season, and invited his host to shoot pheasants on his estates in the South. The amusements of life, he argued, should be accepted with the same philosophy as its ills.

It had been a bad day. A heavy rain had made the moor so spongy that it fairly sprang beneath the feet. Whether or not the grouse had haunts of their own, wherein they were immune from rheumatism, the bag had been small. The women, too, were an unusually dull lot, with the exception of a new-minded *débutante* who bothered Weigall at dinner by demanding the verbal restoration of the vague paintings on the vaulted roof above them.

But it was no one of these things that sat on Weigall's mind as, when the other men went up to bed, he let himself out of the castle and sauntered down to the river. His intimate friend, the companion of his boyhood, the chum of his college days, his fellow-traveller in many lands, the man for whom he possessed stronger affection than for all men, had mysteriously disappeared two days ago, and his track might have sprung to the upper air for all trace he had left behind him. He had been a guest on the adjoining estate during the past week, shooting with the fervour of the true sportsman, making love in the intervals to Adeline Cavan, and apparently in the best of spirits. As far as was known there was nothing to lower his mental mercury, for his rent-roll was a large one, Miss Cavan blushed whenever he looked

* "The Striding Place" first appeared in an earlier version as "The Twins" in the 20 June 1896 issue of *The Speaker* and as "The Striding Place" in *The Smart Set* in July 1900. It was later included in Atherton's collection *The Bell in the Fog and Other Stories* (New York and London: Harper & Brothers, 1905). The current text is based on the 1905 edition. Obvious typographical errors and inconsistencies have been silently corrected.

at her, and, being one of the best shots in England, he was never happier than in August. The suicide theory was preposterous, all agreed, and there was as little reason to believe him murdered. Nevertheless, he had walked out of March Abbey two nights ago without hat or overcoat, and had not been seen since.

The country was being patrolled night and day. A hundred keepers and work-men were beating the woods and poking the bogs on the moors, but as yet not so much as a handkerchief had been found.

Weigall did not believe for a moment that Wyatt Gifford was dead, and al-though it was impossible not to be affected by the general uneasiness, he was disposed to be more angry than frightened. At Cambridge Gifford had been an incorrigible practical joker, and by no means had outgrown the habit; it would be like him to cut across the country in his evening clothes, board a cattle-train, and amuse himself touching up the picture of the sensation in West Riding.

However, Weigall's affection for his friend was too deep to companion with tranquillity in the present state of doubt, and, instead of going to bed early with the other men, he determined to walk until ready for sleep. He went down to the river and followed the path through the woods. There was no moon, but the stars sprinkled their cold light upon the pretty belt of water flowing placidly past wood and ruin, between green masses of overhanging rocks or sloping banks tangled with tree and shrub, leaping occasionally over stones with the harsh notes of an angry scold, to recover its equanimity the moment the way was clear again.

It was very dark in the depths where Weigall trod. He smiled as he recalled a remark of Gifford's: "An English wood is like a good many other things in life— very promising at a distance, but a hollow mockery when you get within. You see daylight on both sides, and the sun freckles the very bracken. Our woods need the night to make them seem what they ought to be—what they once were, before our ancestors' descendants demanded so much more money, in these so much more various days."

Weigall strolled along, smoking, and thinking of his friend, his pranks— many of which had done more credit to his imagination than this—and recall-ing conversations that had lasted the night through. Just before the end of the London season they had walked the streets one hot night after a party, discussing the various theories of the soul's destiny. That afternoon they had met at the coffin of a college friend whose mind had been a blank for the past three years. Some months previously they had called at the asylum to see him. His expression had been senile, his face imprinted with the record of debauchery. In death the face was placid, intelligent, without ignoble lineation—the face of the man they had known at college. Weigall and Gifford had had no time to comment there, and the afternoon and evening were full; but, coming forth from the house of festivity together, they had reverted almost at once to the topic.

"I cherish the theory," Gifford had said, "that the soul sometimes lingers in the body after death. During madness, of course, it is an impotent prisoner, albeit a conscious one. Fancy its agony, and its horror! What more natural than that, when the life-spark goes out, the tortured soul should take possession of the vacant skull and triumph once more for a few hours while old friends look their last? It has had time to repent while compelled to crouch and behold the result of its work, and it has shrived itself into a state of comparative purity. If I had my way, I should stay inside my bones until the coffin had gone into its niche, that I might obviate for my poor old comrade the tragic impersonality of death. And I should like to see justice done to it, as it were—to see it lowered among its ancestors with the ceremony and solemnity that are its due. I am afraid that if I dissevered myself too quickly, I should yield to curiosity and hasten to investigate the mysteries of space."

"You believe in the soul as an independent entity, then—that it and the vital principle are not one and the same?"

"Absolutely. The body and soul are twins, life comrades—sometimes friends, sometimes enemies, but always loyal in the last instance. Some day, when I am tired of the world, I shall go to India and become a mahatma, solely for the pleasure of receiving proof during life of this independent relationship."

"Suppose you were not sealed up properly, and returned after one of your astral flights to find your earthly part unfit for habitation? It is an experiment I don't think I should care to try, unless even juggling with soul and flesh had palled."

"That would not be an uninteresting predicament. I should rather enjoy experimenting with broken machinery."

The high wild roar of water smote suddenly upon Weigall's ear and checked his memories. He left the wood and walked out on the huge slippery stones which nearly close the River Wharfe at this point, and watched the waters boil down into the narrow pass with their furious untiring energy. The black quiet of the woods rose high on either side. The stars seemed colder and whiter just above. On either hand the perspective of the river might have run into a rayless cavern. There was no lonelier spot in England, nor one which had the right to claim so many ghosts, if ghosts there were.

Weigall was not a coward, but he recalled uncomfortably the tales of those that had been done to death in the Strid.[†] Wordsworth's Boy of Egremond had been disposed of by the practical Whitaker; but countless others, more venturesome than wise, had gone down into that narrow boiling course, never to appear in the still pool a few yards beyond. Below the great rocks which form the walls of the Strid was believed to be a natural vault, on to whose shelves the dead were drawn. The spot had an ugly fascination. Weigall stood, visioning skeletons, uncoffined and green, the home of the eyeless things which had devoured all that had covered and filled that rattling symbol of man's mortality; then fell to wondering if any one had attempted to leap the Strid of late. It was covered with slime; he had never seen it look so treacherous.

He shuddered and turned away, impelled, despite his manhood, to flee the spot. As he did so, something tossing in the foam below the fall—something as white, yet independent of it—caught his eye and arrested his step. Then he saw that it was describing a contrary motion to the rushing water—an upward backward motion. Weigall stood rigid, breathless; he fancied he heard the crackling of his hair. Was that a hand? It thrust itself still higher above the boiling foam, turned sidewise, and four frantic fingers were distinctly visible against the black rock beyond.

Weigall's superstitious terror left him. A man was there, struggling to free himself from the suction beneath the Strid, swept down, doubtless, but a moment before his arrival, perhaps as he stood with his back to the current.

He stepped as close to the edge as he dared. The hand doubled as if in imprecation, shaking savagely in the face of that force which leaves its creatures to immutable law; then spread wide again, clutching, expanding, crying for help as audibly as the human voice.

Weigall dashed to the nearest tree, dragged and twisted off a branch with his strong arms, and returned as swiftly to the Strid. The hand was in the same place, still gesticulating as wildly; the body was undoubtedly caught in the rocks below,

---

[†]   "This striding place is called the 'Strid,'
            A name which it took of yore;
        A thousand years hath it borne the name,
            And it shall a thousand more." [Atherton's note]

perhaps already half-way along one of those hideous shelves. Weigall let himself down upon a lower rock, braced his shoulder against the mass beside him, then, leaning out over the water, thrust the branch into the hand. The fingers clutched it convulsively. Weigall tugged powerfully, his own feet dragged perilously near the edge. For a moment he produced no impression, then an arm shot above the waters.

The blood sprang to Weigall's head; he was choked with the impression that the Strid had him in her roaring hold, and he saw nothing. Then the mist cleared. The hand and arm were nearer, although the rest of the body was still concealed by the foam. Weigall peered out with distended eyes. The meagre light revealed in the cuffs links of a peculiar device. The fingers clutching the branch were as familiar.

Weigall forgot the slippery stones, the terrible death if he stepped too far. He pulled with passionate will and muscle. Memories flung themselves into the hot light of his brain, trooping rapidly upon each other's heels, as in the thought of the drowning. Most of the pleasures of his life, good and bad, were identified in some way with this friend. Scenes of college days, of travel, where they had deliberately sought adventure and stood between one another and death upon more occasions than one, of hours of delightful companionship among the treasures of art, and others in the pursuit of pleasure, flashed like the changing particles of a kaleidoscope. Weigall had loved several women; but he would have flouted in these moments the thought that he had ever loved any woman as he loved Wyatt Gifford. There were so many charming women in the world, and in the thirty-two years of his life he had never known another man to whom he had cared to give his intimate friendship.

He threw himself on his face. His wrists were cracking, the skin was torn from his hands. The fingers still gripped the stick. There was life in them yet.

Suddenly something gave way. The hand swung about, tearing the branch from Weigall's grasp. The body had been liberated and flung outward, though still submerged by the foam and spray.

Weigall scrambled to his feet and sprang along the rocks, knowing that the danger from suction was over and that Gifford must be carried straight to the quiet pool. Gifford was a fish in the water and could live under it longer than most men. If he survived this, it would not be the first time that his pluck and science had saved him from drowning.

Weigall reached the pool. A man in his evening clothes floated on it, his face turned towards a projecting rock over which his arm had fallen, upholding the body. The hand that had held the branch hung limply over the rock, its white reflection visible in the black water. Weigall plunged into the shallow pool, lifted Gifford in his arms and returned to the bank. He laid the body down and threw off his coat that he might be the freer to practise the methods of resuscitation. He was glad of the moment's respite. The valiant life in the man might have been exhausted in that last struggle. He had not dared to look at his face, to put his ear to the heart. The hesitation lasted but a moment. There was no time to lose.

He turned to his prostrate friend. As he did so, something strange and disagreeable smote his senses. For a half-moment he did not appreciate its nature. Then his teeth clacked together, his feet, his outstretched arms pointed towards the woods. But he sprang to the side of the man and bent down and peered into his face. There was no face.

THE PRAYER*

Violet Hunt

I

*"It is but giving over of a game,
That must be lost."*—PHILASTER.

"Come, Mrs. Arne—come, my dear, you must not give way like this! You can't stand it—you really can't! Let Miss Kate take you away—now do!" urged the nurse, with her most motherly of intonations.

"Yes, Alice, Mrs. Joyce is right. Come away—do come away—you are only making yourself ill. It is all over; you can do nothing! Oh, oh, do come away!" implored Mrs. Arne's sister, shivering with excitement and nervousness.

A few moments ago Dr. Graham had relinquished his hold on the pulse of Edward Arne with the hopeless movement of the eyebrows that meant—the end.

The nurse had made the little gesture of resignation that was possibly a matter of form with her. The young sister-in-law had hidden her face in her hands. The wife had screamed a scream that had turned them all hot and cold—and flung herself on the bed over her dead husband. There she lay; her cries were terrible, her sobs shook her whole body.

The three gazed at her pityingly, not knowing what to do next. The nurse, folding her hands, looked towards the doctor for directions, and the doctor drummed with his fingers on the bed-post. The young girl timidly stroked the shoulder that heaved and writhed under her touch.

"Go away! Go away!" her sister reiterated continually, in a voice hoarse with fatigue and passion.

"Leave her alone, Miss Kate," whispered the nurse at last; "she will work it off

---

* An earlier version of "The Prayer" appeared as "The Story of a Ghost" in the Christmas Number of *Chapman's Magazine of Fiction* in December 1895. The story was later collected in Hunt's volume of supernatural fiction, *Tales of the Uneasy* (London: Heinemann, 1911). The current text is based on the 1911 edition. Obvious typographical errors and inconsistencies have been silently corrected.

best herself, perhaps."

She turned down the lamp, as if to draw a veil over the scene. Mrs. Arne raised herself on her elbow, showing a face stained with tears and purple with emotion.

"What! Not gone?" she said harshly. "Go away, Kate, go away! It is my house. I don't want you, I want no one—I want to speak to my husband. Will you go away—all of you. Give me an hour, half-an-hour—five minutes!"

She stretched out her arms imploringly to the doctor.

"Well…" said he, almost to himself.

He signed to the two women to withdraw, and followed them out into the passage. "Go and get something to eat," he said peremptorily, "while you can. We shall have trouble with her presently. I'll wait in the dressing-room."

He glanced at the twisting figure on the bed, shrugged his shoulders, and passed into the adjoining room, without, however, closing the door of communication. Sitting down in an arm-chair drawn up to the fire, he stretched himself and closed his eyes. The professional aspects of the case of Edward Arne rose up before him in all its interesting forms of complication…

*   *   *

It was just this professional attitude that Mrs. Arne unconsciously resented both in the doctor and in the nurse. Through all their kindness she had realized and resented their scientific interest in her husband, for to them he had been no more than a curious and complicated case; and now that the blow had fallen, she regarded them both in the light of executioners. Her one desire, expressed with all the shameless sincerity of blind and thoughtless misery, was to be free of their hateful presence and alone—alone with her dead!

She was weary of the doctor's subdued manly tones—of the nurse's commonplace motherliness, too habitually adapted to the needs of all to be appreciated by the individual—of the childish consolation of the young sister, who had never loved, never been married, did not know what sorrow was! Their expressions of sympathy struck her like blows, the touch of their hands on her body, as they tried to raise her, stung her in every nerve.

With a sigh of relief she buried her head in the pillow, pressed her body more closely against that of her husband, and lay motionless.

Her sobs ceased.

* * *

The lamp went out with a gurgle. The fire leaped up, and died. She raised her head and stared about her helplessly, then sinking down again she put her lips to the ear of the dead man.

"Edward—dear Edward!" she whispered, "why have you left me? Darling, why have you left me? I can't stay behind—you know I can't. I am too young to be left. It is only a year since you married me. I never thought it was only for a year. 'Till death us do part!' Yes, I know that's in it, but nobody ever thinks of that! I never thought of living without you! I meant to die with you...

"No—no—I can't die—I must not—till my baby is born. You will never see it. Don't you want to see it? Don't you? Oh, Edward, speak! Say something, darling, one word—one little word! Edward! Edward! are you there? Answer me for God's sake, answer me!

"Darling, I am so tired of waiting. Oh, think, dearest. There is so little time. They only gave me half-an-hour. In half-an-hour they will come and take you away from me—take you where I can't come to you—with all my love I can't come to you! I know the place—I saw it once. A great lonely place full of graves, and little stunted trees dripping with dirty London rain...and gas-lamps flaring all round...but quite, quite dark where the grave is...a long grey stone just like the rest. How could you stay there?—all alone—all alone—without me?

"Do you remember, Edward, what we once said—that whichever of us died first should come back to watch over the other, in the spirit? I promised you, and you promised me. What children we were! Death is not what we thought. It comforted us to say that then.

"Now, it's nothing—nothing—worse than nothing! I don't want your spirit—I can't see it—or feel it—I want you, you, your eyes that looked at me, your mouth that kissed me——"

She raised his arms and clasped them round her neck, and lay there very still, murmuring, "Oh, hold me, hold me! Love me if you can. Am I hateful? This is me! These are your arms..."

The doctor in the next room moved in his chair. The noise awoke her from her dream of contentment, and she unwound the dead arm from her neck, and, holding it up by the wrist, considered it ruefully.

"Yes, I can put it round me, but I have to hold it there. It is quite cold—it doesn't care. Ah, my dear, you don't care! You are dead. I kiss you, but you don't kiss me. Edward! Edward! Oh, for heaven's sake kiss me once. Just once!

"No, no, that won't do—that's not enough! that's nothing! worse than nothing! I want you back, you, all you…What shall I do?…I often pray…Oh, if there be a God in heaven, and if He ever answered a prayer, let Him answer mine—my only prayer. I'll never ask another—and give you back to me! As you were—as I loved you—as I adored you! He must listen. He must! My God, my God, he's mine—he's my husband, he's my lover—give him back to me!"

* * *

"Left alone for half-an-hour or more with the corpse! It's not right!"

The muttered expression of the nurse's revolted sense of professional decency came from the head of the staircase, where she had been waiting for the last few minutes. The doctor joined her.

"Hush, Mrs. Joyce! I'll go to her now."

The door creaked on its hinges as he gently pushed it open and went in.

"What's that? What's that?" screamed Mrs. Arne. "Doctor! Doctor! Don't touch me! Either I am dead or he is alive!"

"Do you want to kill yourself, Mrs. Arne?" said Dr. Graham, with calculated sternness, coming forward; "come away!"

"Not dead! Not dead!" she murmured.

"He is dead, I assure you. Dead and cold an hour ago! Feel!" He took hold of her, as she lay face downwards, and in so doing he touched the dead man's cheek—it was not cold! Instinctively his finger sought a pulse.

"Stop! Wait!" he cried in his intense excitement. "My dear Mrs. Arne, control yourself!"

But Mrs. Arne had fainted, and fallen heavily off the bed on the other side. Her sister, hastily summoned, attended to her, while the man they had all given over for dead was, with faint gasps and sighs and reluctant moans, pulled, as it were, hustled and dragged back over the threshold of life.

II

"Why do you always wear black, Alice?" asked Esther Graham. "You are not in mourning that I know of."

She was Dr. Graham's only daughter and Mrs. Arne's only friend. She sat with Mrs. Arne in the dreary drawing-room of the house in Chelsea. She had come to tea. She was the only person who ever did come to tea there.

She was brusque, kind, and blunt, and had a talent for making inappropriate remarks. Six years ago Mrs. Arne had been a widow for an hour! Her husband had succumbed to an apparently mortal illness, and for the space of an hour had lain dead. When suddenly and inexplicably he had revived from his trance, the shock, combined with six weeks' nursing, had nearly killed his wife. All this Esther had heard from her father. She herself had only come to know Mrs. Arne after her child was born, and all the tragic circumstances of her husband's illness put aside, and it was hoped forgotten. And when her idle question received no answer from the pale absent woman who sat opposite, with listless lack-lustre eyes fixed on the green and blue flames dancing in the fire, she hoped it had passed unnoticed. She waited for five minutes for Mrs. Arne to resume the conversation, then her natural impatience got the better of her.

"Do say something, Alice!" she implored.

"Esther, I beg your pardon!" said Mrs. Arne. "I was thinking."

"What were you thinking of?"

"I don't know."

"No, of course you don't. People who sit and stare into the fire never do think, really. They are only brooding and making themselves ill, and that is what you are doing. You mope, you take no interest in anything, you never go out—I am sure you have not been out of doors today?"

"No—yes—I believe not. It is so cold."

"You are sure to feel the cold if you sit in the house all day, and sure to get ill! Just look at yourself!"

Mrs. Arne rose and looked at herself in the Italian mirror over the chimney-piece. It reflected faithfully enough her even pallor, her dark hair and eyes, the sweeping length of her eyelashes, the sharp curves of her nostrils, and the delicate arch of her eyebrows, that formed a thin sharp black line, so clear as to seem almost unnatural.

"Yes, I do look ill," she said with conviction.

"No wonder. You choose to bury yourself alive."

"Sometimes I do feel as if I lived in a grave. I look up at the ceiling and fancy it is my coffin-lid."

"Don't please talk like that!" expostulated Miss Graham, pointing to Mrs. Arne's little girl. "If only for Dolly's sake, I think you should not give way to such morbid fancies. It isn't good for her to see you like this always."

"Oh, Esther," the other exclaimed, stung into something like vivacity, "don't reproach me! I hope I am a good mother to my child!"

"Yes, dear, you are a model mother—and model wife too. Father says the way you look after your husband is something wonderful, but don't you think for your own sake you might try to be a little gayer? You encourage these moods, don't you? What is it? Is it the house?"

She glanced around her—at the high ceiling, at the heavy damask portieres, the tall cabinets of china, the dim oak panelling—it reminded her of a neglected museum. Her eye travelled into the farthest corners, where the faint filmy dusk was already gathering, lit only by the bewildering cross-lights of the glass panels of cabinet doors—to the tall narrow windows—then back again to the woman in her mourning dress, cowering by the fire. She said sharply—

"You should go out more."

"I do not like to—leave my husband."

"Oh, I know that he is delicate and all that, but still, does he never permit you to leave him? Does he never go out by himself?"

"Not often!"

"And you have no pets! It is very odd of you. I simply can't imagine a house without animals!"

"We did have a dog once," answered Mrs. Arne plaintively, "but it howled so we had to give it away. It would not go near Edward…But please don't imagine that I am dull! I have my child." She laid her hand on the flaxen head at her knee.

Miss Graham rose, frowning.

"Ah, you are too bad!" she exclaimed. "You are like a widow exactly, with one child, stroking its orphan head and saying, 'Poor fatherless darling.'"

Voices were heard outside. Miss Graham stopped talking quite suddenly, and sought her veil and gloves on the mantelpiece.

"You need not go, Esther," said Mrs. Arne. "It is only my husband."

"Oh, but it is getting late," said the other, crumpling up her gloves in her muff, and shuffling her feet nervously.

"Come!" said her hostess, with a bitter smile, "put your gloves on properly—if you must go—but it is quite early still."

"Please don't go, Miss Graham," put in the child.

"I must. Go and meet your papa, like a good girl."

"I don't want to."

"You mustn't talk like that, Dolly," said the doctor's daughter absently, still looking towards the door. Mrs. Arne rose and fastened the clasps of the big fur-cloak for her friend. The wife's white, sad, oppressed face came very close to the girl's cheerful one, as she murmured in a low voice—

"You don't like my husband, Esther? I can't help noticing it. Why don't you?"

"Nonsense!" retorted the other, with the emphasis of one who is repelling an overtrue accusation. "I do, only——"

"Only what?"

"Well, dear, it is foolish of me, of course, but I am—a little afraid of him."

"Afraid of Edward!" said his wife slowly. "Why should you be?"

"Well, dear—you see—I—I suppose women can't help being a little afraid of their friends' husbands—they can spoil their friendships with their wives in a moment, if they choose to disapprove of them. I really must go! Good-bye, child; give me a kiss! Don't ring, Alice. Please don't! I can open the door for myself——"

"Why should you?" said Mrs. Arne. "Edward is in the hall; I heard him speaking to Foster."

"No; he has gone into his study. Good-bye, you apathetic creature!" She gave Mrs. Arne a brief kiss and dashed out of the room. The voices outside had ceased, and she had reasonable hopes of reaching the door without being intercepted by Mrs. Arne's husband. But he met her on the stairs. Mrs. Arne, listening intently from her seat by the fire, heard her exchange a few shy sentences with him, the sound of which died away as they went downstairs together. A few moments after, Edward Arne came into the room and dropped into the chair just vacated by his wife's visitor.

He crossed his legs and said nothing. Neither did she.

His nearness had the effect of making the woman look at once several years older. Where she was pale he was well-coloured; the network of little filmy wrinkles that, on a close inspection, covered her face, had no parallel on his smooth skin. He was handsome; soft, well-groomed flakes of auburn hair lay over his forehead, and his steely blue eyes shone equably, a contrast to the sombre fire of hers, and the masses of dark crinkly hair that shaded her brow. The deep lines of permanent discontent furrowed that brow as she sat with her chin propped on her hands, and her elbows resting on her knees. Neither spoke. When the hands of the clock over Mrs. Arne's head pointed to seven, the white-aproned figure of the nurse appeared in the doorway, and the little girl rose and kissed her mother very tenderly.

Mrs. Arne's forehead contracted. Looking uneasily at her husband, she said to the child tentatively, yet boldly, as one grasps the nettle, "Say good-night to your father!"

The child obeyed, saying, "Good-night" indifferently in her father's direction.

"Kiss him!"

"No, please—please not."

Her mother looked down on her curiously, sadly....

"You are a naughty, spoilt child!" she said, but without conviction. "Excuse her, Edward."

He did not seem to have heard.

"Well, if you don't care——" said his wife bitterly. "Come, child!" She caught the little girl by the hand and left the room.

At the door she half turned and looked fixedly at her husband. It was a strange ambiguous gaze; in it passion and dislike were strangely combined. Then she shivered and closed the door softly after her.

The man in the arm-chair sat with no perceptible change of attitude, his unspeculative eyes fixed on the fire, his hands clasped idly in front of him. The pose was obviously habitual. The servant brought lights and closed the shutters, drew the curtains, and made up the fire noisily, without, however, eliciting any reproof from his master.

Edward Arne was an ideal master, as far as Foster was concerned. He kept cases of cigars, but never smoked them, although the supply had often to be renewed. He did not care what he ate or drank, although he kept as good a cellar as most gentlemen—Foster knew that. He never interfered, he counted for nothing, he gave no trouble. Foster had no intention of ever leaving such an easy place. True, his master was not cordial; he very seldom addressed him or seemed to know whether he was there, but then neither did he grumble if the fire in the study was allowed to go out, or interfere with Foster's liberty in any way. He had a better place of it than Annette, Mrs. Arne's maid, who would be called up in the middle of the night to bathe her mistress's forehead with eau-de-Cologne, or made to brush her long hair for hours together to soothe her. Naturally enough

Foster and Annette compared notes as to their respective situations, and drew unflattering parallels between this capricious wife and model husband.

III

Miss Graham was not a demonstrative woman. On her return home she somewhat startled her father, as he sat by his study table, deeply interested in his diagnosis book, by the sudden violence of her embrace.

"Why this excitement?" he asked, smiling and turning round. He was a young-looking man for his age; his thin wiry figure and clear colour belied the evidence of his hair, tinged with grey, and the tired wrinkles that gave value to the acuteness and brilliancy of the eyes they surrounded.

"I don't know!" she replied, "only you are so nice and alive somehow. I always feel like this when I come back from seeing the Arnes."

"Then don't go to see the Arnes."

"I'm so fond of her, father, and she will never come here to me, as you know. Or else nothing would induce me to enter her tomb of a house, and talk to that walking funeral of a husband of hers. I managed to get away today without having to shake hands with him. I always try to avoid it. But, father, I do wish you would go and see Alice."

"Is she ill?"

"Well, not exactly ill, I suppose, but her eyes make me quite uncomfortable, and she says such odd things! I don't know if it is you or the clergyman she wants, but she is all wrong somehow! She never goes out except to church; she never pays a call, or has any one to call on her! Nobody ever asks the Arnes to dinner, and I'm sure I don't blame them—the sight of that man at one's table would spoil any party—and they never entertain. She is always alone. Day after day I go in and find her sitting over the fire, with that same brooding expression. I shouldn't be surprised in the least if she were to go mad some day. Father, what is it? What is the tragedy of the house? There is one I am convinced. And yet, though I have been the intimate friend of that woman for years, I know no more about her than the man in the street."

"She keeps her skeleton safe in the cupboard," said Dr. Graham. "I respect her for that. And please don't talk nonsense about tragedies. Alice Arne is only morbid—the malady of the age. And she is a very religious woman."

"I wonder if she complains of her odious husband to Mr. Bligh. She is always going to his services."

"Odious?"

"Yes, odious!" Miss Graham shuddered. "I cannot stand him! I cannot bear the touch of his cold froggy hands, and the sight of his fishy eyes! That inane smile of his simply makes me shrivel up. Father, honestly, do you like him yourself?"

"My dear, I hardly know him! It is his wife I have known ever since she was a child, and I a boy at college. Her father was my tutor. I never knew her husband till six years ago, when she called me in to attend him in a very serious illness. I suppose she never speaks of it? No? A very odd affair. For the life of me I cannot tell how he managed to recover. You needn't tell people, for it affects my reputation, but I didn't save him! Indeed I have never been able to account for it. The man was given over for dead!"

"He might as well be dead for all the good he is," said Esther scornfully. "I have never heard him say more than a couple of sentences in my life."

"Yet he was an exceedingly brilliant young man; one of the best men of his year at Oxford—a good deal run after—poor Alice was wild to marry him!"

"In love with that spiritless creature? He is like a house with someone dead in it, and all the blinds down!"

"Come, Esther, don't be morbid—not to say silly! You are very hard on the poor man! What's wrong with him? He is the ordinary, commonplace, cold-blooded specimen of humanity, a little stupid, a little selfish—people who have gone through a serious illness like that are apt to be—but on the whole, a good husband, a good father, a good citizen——"

"Yes, and his wife is afraid of him, and his child hates him!" exclaimed Esther.

"Nonsense!" said Dr. Graham sharply. "The child is spoilt. Only children are apt to be—and the mother wants a change or a tonic of some kind. I'll go and talk to her when I have time. Go along and dress. Have you forgotten that George Graham is coming to dinner?"

After she had gone the doctor made a note on the corner of his blotting-pad, "Mem.: to go and see Mrs. Arne," and dismissed the subject of the memorandum entirely from his mind.

* * *

George Graham was the doctor's nephew, a tall, weedy, cumbrous young man, full of fads and fallacies, with a gentle manner that somehow inspired confidence. He was several years younger than Esther, who loved to listen to his semi-scientific, semi-romantic stories of things met with in the course of his profession. "Oh, I come across very queer things!" he would say mysteriously, "There's a queer little widow——!"

"Tell me about your little widow?" asked Esther that day after dinner, when, her father having gone back to his study, she and her cousin sat together as usual.

He laughed.

"You like to hear of my professional experiences? Well, she certainly interested me," he said thoughtfully. "She is an odd psychological study in her way. I wish I could come across her again."

"Where did you come across her, and what is her name?"

"I don't know her name, I don't want to; she is not a personage to me, only a case. I hardly know her face even. I have never seen it except in the twilight. But I gathered that she lived somewhere in Chelsea, for she came out on to the Embankment with only a kind of lacy thing over her head; she can't live far off, I fancy."

Esther became instantly attentive. "Go on," she said.

"It was three weeks ago," said George Graham. "I was coming along the Embankment about ten o'clock. I walked through that little grove, you know, just between Cheyne Walk and the river, and I heard in there someone sobbing very bitterly. I looked and saw a woman sitting on a seat, with her head in her hands, crying. I was most awfully sorry, of course, and I thought I could perhaps do something for her, get her a glass of water, or salts, or something. I took her for a woman of the people—it was quite dark, you know. So I asked her very politely if I could do anything for her, and then I noticed her hands—they were quite white and covered with diamonds."

"You were sorry you spoke, I suppose," said Esther.

"She raised her head and said—I believe she laughed—'Are you going to tell me to move on?'"

"She thought you were a policeman?"

"Probably—if she thought at all—but she was in a semi-dazed condition. I told her to wait till I came back, and dashed round the corner to the chemist's and bought a bottle of salts. She thanked me, and made a little effort to rise and go away. She seemed very weak. I told her I was a medical man, I started in and talked to her."

"And she to you?"

"Yes, quite straight. Don't you know that women always treat a doctor as if he were one step removed from their father confessor—not human—not in the same category as themselves? It is not complimentary to one as a man, but one hears a good deal one would not otherwise hear. She ended by telling me all about herself—in a veiled way, of course. It soothed her—relieved her—she seemed not to have had an outlet for years!"

"To a mere stranger!"

"To a doctor. And she did not know what she was saying half the time. She was hysterical, of course. Heavens! what nonsense she talked! She spoke of herself as a person somehow haunted, cursed by some malign fate, a victim of some fearful spiritual catastrophe, don't you know? I let her run on. She was convinced of the reality of a sort of 'doom' that she had fancied had befallen her. It was quite pathetic. Then it got rather chilly—she shivered—I suggested her going in. She shrank back; she said, 'If you only knew what a relief it is, how much less miserable I am out here! I can breathe; I can live—it is my only glimpse of the world that is alive—I live in a grave—oh, let me stay!' She seemed positively afraid to go home."

"Perhaps someone bullied her at home."

"I suppose so, but then—she had no husband. He died, she told me, years ago. She had adored him, she said——"

"Is she pretty?"

"Pretty! Well, I hardly noticed. Let me see! Oh, yes, I suppose she was pretty—no, now I think of it, she would be too worn and faded to be what you call pretty."

Esther smiled.

"Well, we sat there together for quite an hour, then the clock of Chelsea church struck eleven, and she got up and said 'Good-bye,' holding out her hand quite naturally, as if our meeting and conversation had been nothing out of the common. There was a sound like a dead leaf trailing across the walk and she was gone."

"Didn't you ask if you should see her again?"

"That would have been a mean advantage to take."

"You might have offered to see her home."

"I saw she did not mean me to."

"She was a lady, you say," pondered Esther. "How was she dressed?"

"Oh, all right, like a lady—in black—mourning, I suppose. She has dark crinkly hair, and her eyebrows are very thin and arched—I noticed that in the dusk."

"Does this photograph remind you of her?" asked Esther suddenly, taking him to the mantelpiece.

"Rather!"

"Alice! Oh, it couldn't be—she is not a widow, her husband is alive—has your friend any children?"

"Yes, one, she mentioned it."

"How old?"

"Six years old, I think she said. She talks of the 'responsibility of bringing up an orphan.'"

"George, what time is it?" Esther asked suddenly.

"About nine o'clock."

"Would you mind coming out with me?"

"I should like it. Where shall we go?"

"To St. Adhelm's! It is close by here. There is a special late service tonight, and Mrs. Arne is sure to be there."

"Oh, Esther—curiosity!"

"No, not mere curiosity. Don't you see if it is my Mrs. Arne who talked to you like this, it is very serious? I have thought her ill for a long time; but as ill as that!——"

At St. Adhelm's Church, Esther Graham pointed out a woman who was kneeling beside a pillar in an attitude of intense devotion and abandonment. She rose from her knees, and turned her rapt face up towards the pulpit whence the Reverend Ralph Bligh was holding his impassioned discourse. George Graham touched his cousin on the shoulder, and motioned to her to leave her place on the outermost rank of worshippers.

"That is the woman!" said he.

IV

"Mem.: to go and see Mrs. Arne." The doctor came across this note in his blotting-pad one day six weeks later. His daughter was out of town. He had heard nothing of the Arnes since her departure. He had promised to go and see her. He was a little conscience-stricken. Yet another week elapsed before he found time to call upon the daughter of his old tutor.

At the corner of Tite Street he met Mrs. Arne's husband, and stopped. A doctor's professional kindliness of manner is, or ought to be, independent of his personal likings and dislikings, and there was a pleasant cordiality about his greeting which should have provoked a corresponding fervour on the part of Edward Arne.

"How are you, Arne?" Graham said. "I was on my way to call on your wife."

"Ah—yes!" said Edward Arne, with the ascending inflection of polite acquiescence. A ray of blue from his eyes rested transitorily on the doctor's face, and in that short moment the latter noted its intolerable vacuity, and for the first time in his life he felt a sharp pang of sympathy for the wife of such a husband.

"I suppose you are off to your club?—er—good-bye!" he wound up abruptly. With the best will in the world he somehow found it almost impossible to carry on a conversation with Edward Arne, who raised his hand to his hat-brim in token of salutation, smiled sweetly, and walked on.

"He really is extraordinarily good-looking," reflected the doctor, as he watched him down the street and safely over the crossing with a certain degree of solicitude for which he could not exactly account. "And yet one feels one's vitality ebbing out at the finger-ends as one talks to him. I shall begin to believe in Esther's absurd fancies about him soon. Ah, there's the little girl!" he exclaimed, as he turned into Cheyne Walk and caught sight of her with her nurse, making violent demonstrations to attract his attention. "She is alive, at any rate. How is your mother, Dolly?" he asked.

"Quite well, thank you," was the child's reply. She added, "She's crying. She sent me away because I looked at her. So I did. Her cheeks are quite red."

"Run away—run away and play!" said the doctor nervously. He ascended the steps of the house, and rang the bell very gently and neatly.

"Not at——" began Foster, with the intonation of polite falsehood, but stopped on seeing the doctor, who, with his daughter, was a privileged person. "Mrs. Arne will see you, Sir."

"Mrs. Arne is not alone?" he said interrogatively.

"Yes, Sir, quite alone. I have just taken tea in."

Dr. Graham's doubts were prompted by the low murmur as of a voice, or voices, which came to him through the open door of the room at the head of the stairs. He paused and listened while Foster stood by, merely remarking, "Mrs. Arne do talk to herself sometimes, Sir."

It was Mrs. Arne's voice—the doctor recognized it now. It was not the voice of a sane or healthy woman. He at once mentally removed his visit from the category of a morning call, and prepared for a semi-professional inquiry.

"Don't announce me," he said to Foster, and quietly entered the back drawing-room, which was separated by a heavy tapestry portiere from the room where Mrs. Arne sat, with an open book on the table before her, from which she had been apparently reading aloud. Her hands were now clasped tightly over her face, and when, presently, she removed them and began feverishly to turn page after page of her book, the crimson of her cheeks was seamed with white where her fingers had impressed themselves.

The doctor wondered if she saw him, for though her eyes were fixed in his direction, there was no apprehension in them. She went on reading, and it was the text, mingled with passionate interjection and fragmentary utterances, of the Burial Service that met his ears.

"'For as in Adam all die!' All die! It says all! For he must reign…. The last enemy that shall be destroyed is Death. What shall they do if the dead rise not at all!… I die daily…! Daily! No, no, better get it over…dead and buried…out of sight, out of mind…under a stone. Dead men don't come back…. Go on! Get it over. I want to hear the earth rattle on the coffin, and then I shall know it is done. 'Flesh and blood cannot inherit!' Oh, what did I do? What have I done? Why did I wish it so fervently? Why did I pray for it so earnestly? God gave me my wish——"

"Alice! Alice!" groaned the doctor.

She looked up. "'When this corruptible shall have put on incorruption——' 'Dust to dust, ashes to ashes, earth to earth——' Yes, that is it. 'After death, though worms destroy this body——'"

She flung the book aside and sobbed.

"That is what I was afraid of. My God! My God! Down there—in the dark—for ever and ever and ever! I could not bear to think of it! My Edward! And so I interfered...and prayed...and prayed till...Oh! I am punished. Flesh and blood could not inherit! I kept him there—I would not let him go.... I kept him.... I prayed.... I denied him Christian burial.... Oh, how could I know...."

"Good heavens, Alice!" said Graham, coming sensibly forward, "what does this mean? I have heard of schoolgirls going through the marriage service by themselves, but the burial service——"

He laid down his hat and went on severely, "What have you to do with such things? Your child is flourishing—your husband alive and here——"

"And who kept him here?" interrupted Alice Arne fiercely, accepting the fact of his appearance without comment.

"You did," he answered quickly, "with your care and tenderness. I believe the warmth of your body, as you lay beside him for that half-hour, maintained the vital heat during that extraordinary suspension of the heart's action, which made us all give him up for dead. You were his best doctor, and brought him back to us."

"Yes, it was I—it was I—you need not tell me it was I!"

"Come, be thankful!" he said cheerfully. "Put that book away, and give me some tea, I'm very cold."

"Oh, Dr. Graham, how thoughtless of me!" said Mrs. Arne, rallying at the slight imputation on her politeness he had purposely made. She tottered to the bell and rang it before he could anticipate her.

"Another cup," she said quite calmly to Foster, who answered it. Then she sat down quivering all over with the suddenness of the constraint put upon her.

"Yes, sit down and tell me all about it," said Dr. Graham good-humouredly, at the same time observing her with the closeness he gave to difficult cases.

"There is nothing to tell," she said simply, shaking her head, and futilely altering the position of the tea-cups on the tray. "It all happened years ago. Nothing can be done now. Will you have sugar?"

He drank his tea and made conversation. He talked to her of some Dante lectures she was attending; of some details connected with her child's Kindergarten classes. These subjects did not interest her. There was a subject she wished to discuss, he could see that a question trembled on her tongue, and tried to lead up to it.

She introduced it herself, quite quietly, over a second cup. "Sugar, Dr.

Graham? I forget. Dr. Graham, tell me, do you believe that prayers—wicked un-reasonable prayers—are granted?"

He helped himself to another slice of bread and butter before answering.

"Well," he said slowly, "it seems hard to believe that every fool who has a voice to pray with, and a brain where to conceive idiotic requests with, should be permitted to interfere with the economy of the universe. As a rule, if people were long-sighted enough to see the result of their petitions, I fancy very few of us would venture to interfere."

Mrs. Arne groaned.

She was a good Churchwoman, Graham knew, and he did not wish to sap her faith in any way, so he said no more, but inwardly wondered if a too rigid interpretation of some of the religious dogmas of the Vicar of St. Adhelm's, her spiritual adviser, was not the clue to her distress. Then she put another question—

"Eh! What?" he said. "Do I believe in ghosts? I will believe you if you will tell me you have seen one."

"You know, Doctor," she went on, "I was always afraid of ghosts—of spir-its—things unseen. I couldn't ever read about them. I could not bear the idea of someone in the room with me that I could not see. There was a text that always frightened me that hung up in my room: 'Thou, God, seest me!' It frightened me when I was a child, whether I had been doing wrong or not. But now," shudder-ing, "I think there are worse things than ghosts."

"Well, now, what sort of things?" he asked good-humouredly. "Astral bodies——?"

She leaned forward and laid her hot hand on his.

"Oh, Doctor, tell me, if a spirit—without the body we know it by—is terri-ble, what of a body"—her voice sank to a whisper, "a body—senseless—lonely—stranded on this earth—without a spirit?"

She was watching his face anxiously. He was divided between a morbid incli-nation to laugh and the feeling of intense discomfort provoked by this wretched scene. He longed to give the conversation a more cheerful turn, yet did not wish to offend her by changing it too abruptly.

"I have heard of people not being able to keep body and soul together," he replied at last, "but I am not aware that practically such a division of forces has ever been achieved. And if we could only accept the theory of the de-spiritualized body, what a number of antipathetic people now wandering about in the world it would account for!"

The piteous gaze of her eyes seemed to seek to ward off the blow of his misplaced jocularity. He left his seat and sat down on the couch beside her.

"Poor child! poor girl! you are ill, you are over-excited. What is it? Tell me," he asked her as tenderly as the father she had lost in early life might have done. Her head sank on his shoulder.

"Are you unhappy?" he asked her gently.

"Yes!"

"You are too much alone. Get your mother or your sister to come and stay with you."

"They won't come," she wailed. "They say the house is like a grave. Edward has made himself a study in the basement. It's an impossible room—but he has moved all his things in, and I can't—I won't go to him there...."

"You're wrong. For it's only a fad," said Graham, "he'll tire of it. And you must see more people somehow. It's a pity my daughter is away. Had you any visitors today?"

"Not a soul has crossed the threshold for eighteen days."

"We must change all that," said the doctor vaguely. "Meantime you must cheer up. Why, you have no need to think of ghosts and graves—no need to be melancholy—you have your husband and your child——"

"I have my child—yes."

The doctor took hold of Mrs. Arne by the shoulder, and held her a little away from him. He thought he had found the cause of her trouble—a more commonplace one than he had supposed.

"I have known you, Alice, since you were a child," he said gravely. "Answer me! You love your husband, don't you?"

"Yes." It was as if she were answering futile prefatory questions in the witness-box. Yet he saw by the intense excitement in her eyes that he had come to the point she feared, and yet desired to bring forward.

"And he loves you?"

She was silent.

"Well, then, if you love each other, what more can you want? Why do you say you have only your child in that absurd way?"

She was still silent, and he gave her a little shake.

"Tell me, have you and he had any difference lately? Is there any—coldness—any—temporary estrangement between you?"

He was hardly prepared for the burst of foolish laughter that proceeded from the demure Mrs. Arne as she rose and confronted him, all the blood in her body seeming for the moment to rush to her usually pale cheeks.

"Coldness! Temporary estrangement! If that were all! Oh, is everyone blind but me? There is all the world between us!—all the difference between this world and the next!"

She sat down again beside the doctor and whispered in his ear, and her words were like a breath of hot wind from some Gehenna of the soul.

"Oh, Doctor, I have borne it for six years, and I must speak. No other woman could bear what I have borne, and yet be alive! And I loved him so; you don't know how I loved him! That was it—that was my crime——"

"Crime?" repeated the doctor.

"Yes, crime! It was impious, don't you see? But I have been punished. Oh, Doctor, you don't know what my life is! Listen! Listen! I must tell you. To live with a—— At first before I guessed when I used to put my arms round him, and he merely submitted—and then it dawned on me what I was kissing! It is enough to turn a living woman into stone—for I am living, though sometimes I forget it. Yes, I am a live woman, though I live in a grave. Think what it is!—to wonder every night if you will be alive in the morning, to lie down every night in an open grave—to smell death in every corner—every room—to breathe death—to touch it...."

The portiere in front of the door shook, a hoopstick parted it, a round white clad bundle supported on a pair of mottled red legs peeped in, pushing a hoop in front of her. The child made no noise. Mrs. Arne seemed to have heard her, however. She slewed round violently as she sat on the sofa beside Dr. Graham, leaving her hot hands clasped in his.

"You ask Dolly," she exclaimed. "She knows it, too—she feels it."

"No, no, Alice, this won't do!" the doctor adjured her very low. Then he raised his voice and ordered the child from the room. He had managed to lift Mrs. Arne's feet and laid her full length on the sofa by the time the maid reappeared. She had fainted.

He pulled down her eyelids and satisfied himself as to certain facts he had up till now dimly apprehended. When Mrs. Arne's maid returned, he gave her mistress over to her care and proceeded to Edward Arne's new study in the basement.

"Morphia!" he muttered to himself, as he stumbled and faltered through gaslit passages, where furtive servants eyed him and scuttled to their burrows.

"What is he burying himself down here for?" he thought. "Is it to get out of her way? They *are* a nervous pair of them!"

* * *

Arne was sunk in a large arm-chair drawn up before the fire. There was no other light, except a faint reflection from the gas-lamp in the road, striking down past the iron bars of the window that was sunk below the level of the street. The room was comfortless and empty, there was little furniture in it except a large bookcase at Arne's right hand and a table with a Tantalus on it standing some way off. There was a faded portrait in pastel of Alice Arne over the mantelpiece, and beside it, a poor pendant, a pen and ink sketch of the master of the house. They were quite discrepant, in size and medium, but they appeared to look at each other with the stolid attentiveness of newly married people.

"Seedy, Arne?" Graham said.

"Rather, today. Poke the fire for me, will you?"

"I've known you quite seven years," said the doctor cheerfully, "so I presume I can do that…. There, now!… And I'll presume further—— What have we got here?"

He took a small bottle smartly out of Edward Arne's fingers and raised his eyebrows. Edward Arne had rendered it up agreeably; he did not seem upset or annoyed.

"Morphia. It isn't a habit. I only got hold of the stuff yesterday—found it about the house. Alice was very jumpy all day, and communicated her nerves to me, I suppose. I've none as a rule, but do you know, Graham, I seem to be getting them—feel things a good deal more than I did, and want to talk about them."

"What, are you growing a soul?" said the doctor carelessly, lighting a cigarette.

"Heaven forbid!" Arne answered equably. "I've done very well without it all these years. But I'm fond of old Alice, you know, in my own way. When I was a young man, I was quite different. I took things hardly and got excited about them. Yes, excited. I was wild about Alice, wild! Yes, by Jove! though she has forgotten all about it."

"Not that, but still it's natural she should long for some little demonstration of affection now and then…and she'd be awfully distressed if she saw you fooling with that bottle of morphia! You know, Arne, after that narrow squeak you had of it five years ago, Alice and I have a good right to consider that your life belongs to us!"

Edward Arne settled in his chair and replied, rather fretfully—

"All very well, but you didn't manage to do the job thoroughly. You didn't turn me out lively enough to please Alice. She's annoyed because when I take her in my arms, I don't hold her tight enough. I'm too quiet, too languid!… Hang it all, Graham, I believe she'd like me to stand for Parliament!… Why can't she let me just go along my own way? Surely a man who's come through an illness like mine can be let off parlour tricks? All this worry—it culminated the other day when I said I wanted to colonize a room down here, and did, with a spurt that took it out of me horribly—all this worry, I say, seeing her upset and so on, keeps me low, and so I feel as if I wanted to take drugs to soothe me."

"Soothe!" said Graham. "This stuff is more than soothing if you take enough of it. I'll send you something more like what you want, and I'll take this away, by your leave."

"I really can't argue!" replied Arne…. "If you see Alice, tell her you find me fairly comfortable and don't put her off this room. I really like it best. She can come and see me here, I keep a good fire, tell her…. I feel as if I wanted to sleep…" he added brusquely.

"You have been indulging already," said Graham softly. Arne had begun to doze off. His cushion had sagged down, the doctor stooped to rearrange it, carelessly laying the little phial for the moment in a crease of the rug covering the man's knees.

*   *   *

Mrs. Arne in her mourning dress was crossing the hall as he came to the top of the basement steps and pushed open the swing door. She was giving some orders to Foster, the butler, who disappeared as the doctor advanced.

"You're about again," he said, "good girl!"

"Too silly of me," she said, "to be hysterical! After all these years! One should be able to keep one's own counsel. But it is over now, I promise I will never speak of it again."

"We frightened poor Dolly dreadfully. I had to order her out like a regiment of soldiers."

"Yes, I know. I'm going to her now."

On his suggestion that she should look in on her husband first she looked askance.

"Down there!"

"Yes, that's his fancy. Let him be. He is a good deal depressed about himself and you. He notices a great deal more than you think. He isn't quite as apathetic as you describe him to be.... Come here!" He led her into the unlit dining-room a little way. "You expect too much, my dear. You do really! You make too many demands on the vitality you saved."

"What did one save him for?" she asked fiercely. She continued more quietly, "I know. I am going to be different."

"Not you," said Graham fondly. He was very partial to Alice Arne in spite of her silliness. "You'll worry about Edward till the end of the chapter. I know you. And"—he turned her round by the shoulder so that she fronted the light in the hall—"you elusive thing, let me have a good look at you.... Hum! Your eyes, they're a bit starey...."

He let her go again with a sigh of impotence. Something must be done... soon...he must think...He got hold of his coat and began to get into it....

Mrs. Arne smiled, buttoned a button for him and then opened the front door, like a good hostess, a very little way. With a quick flirt of his hat he was gone, and she heard the clap of his brougham door and the order "Home."

*   *   *

"Been saying good-bye to that thief Graham?" said her husband gently, when she entered his room, her pale eyes staring a little, her thin hand busy at the front of her dress....

"Thief? Why? One moment! Where's your switch?"

She found it and turned on a blaze of light from which her husband seemed to shrink.

"Well, he carried off my drops. Afraid of my poisoning myself, I suppose?"

"Or acquiring the morphia habit," said his wife in a dull level voice, "as I have."

She paused. He made no comment. Then, picking up the little phial Dr. Graham had left in the crease of the rug, she spoke—

"You are the thief, Edward, as it happens, this is mine."

"Is it? I found it knocking about: I didn't know it was yours. Well, will you give me some?"

"I will, if you like."

"Well, dear, decide. You know I am in your hands and Graham's. He was rubbing that into me today."

"Poor lamb!" she said derisively; "I'd not allow my doctor, or my wife either, to dictate to me whether I should put an end to myself, or not."

"Ah, but you've got a spirit, you see!" Arne yawned. "However, let me have a go at the stuff and then you put it on top of the wardrobe or a shelf, where I shall know it is, but never reach out to get it, I promise you."

"No, you wouldn't reach out a hand to keep yourself alive, let alone kill yourself," said she. "That is you all over, Edward."

"And don't you see that is why I did die," he said, with earnestness unexpected by her. "And then, unfortunately, you and Graham bustled up and wouldn't let Nature take its course…. I rather wish you hadn't been so officious."

"And let you stay dead," said she carelessly. "But at the time I cared for you so much that I should have had to kill myself, or commit suttee like a Bengali widow. Ah, well!"

She reached out for a glass half-full of water that stood on the low ledge of a bookcase close by the arm of his chair…. "Will this glass do? What's in it? Only water? How much morphia shall I give you? An overdose?"

"I don't care if you do, and that's a fact."

"It was a joke, Edward," she said piteously.

"No joke to me. This fag end of life I've clawed hold of, doesn't interest me. And I'm bound to be interested in what I'm doing or I'm no good. I'm no earthly good now. I don't enjoy life, I've nothing to enjoy it with—in here"—he struck his breast. "It's like a dull party one goes to by accident. All I want to do is to get into a cab and go home."

His wife stood over him with the half-full glass in one hand and the little bottle in the other. Her eyes dilated…her chest heaved….

"Edward!" she breathed. "Was it all so useless?"

"Was what useless? Yes, as I was telling you, I go as one in a dream—a bad,

bad dream, like the dreams I used to have when I overworked at college. I was brilliant, Alice, brilliant, do you hear? At some cost, I expect! Now I hate people— my fellow creatures. I've left them. They come and go, jostling me, and pushing me, on the pavements as I go along, avoiding them. Do you know where they should be, really, in relation to me?"

He rose a little in his seat—she stepped nervously aside, made as if to put down the bottle and the glass she was holding, then thought better of it and continued to extend them mechanically.

"They should be over my head. I've already left them and their petty nonsense of living. They mean nothing to me, no more than if they were ghosts walking. Or perhaps it's I who am a ghost to them?... You don't understand it. It's because I suppose you have no imagination. You just know what you want and do your best to get it. You blurt out your blessed petition to your Deity and the idea that you're irrelevant never enters your head, soft, persistent, High Church thing that you are!..."

Alice Arne smiled, and balanced the objects she was holding. He motioned her to pour out the liquid from one to the other, but she took no heed; she was listening with all her ears. It was the nearest approach to the language of compliment, to anything in the way of loverlike personalities that she had heard fall from his lips since his illness. He went on, becoming as it were lukewarm to his subject—

"But the worst of it is that once break the cord that links you to humanity—it can't be mended. Man doesn't live by bread alone...or lives to disappoint you. What am I to you, without my own poor personality?... Don't stare so, Alice! I haven't talked so much or so intimately for ages, have I? Let me try and have it out.... Are you in any sort of hurry?"

"No, Edward."

"Pour that stuff out and have done.... Well, Alice, it's a queer feeling, I tell you. One goes about with one's looks on the ground, like a man who eyes the bed he is going to lie down in, and longs for. Alice, the crust of the earth seems a barrier between me and my own place. I want to scratch the boardings with my nails and shriek something like this: 'Let me get down to you all, there where I belong!' It's a horrible sensation, like a vampire reversed!..."

"Is that why you insisted on having this room in the basement?" she asked breathlessly.

"Yes, I can't bear being upstairs, somehow. Here, with these barred windows and stone-cold floors…I can see the people's feet walking above there in the street…one has some sort of illusion…."

"Oh!" She shivered and her eyes travelled like those of a caged creature round the bare room and fluttered when they rested on the sombre windows imperiously barred. She dropped her gaze to the stone flags that showed beyond the oasis of Turkey carpet on which Arne's chair stood…. Then to the door, the door that she had closed on entering. It had heavy bolts, but they were not drawn against her, though by the look of her eyes it seemed she half imagined they were….

She made a step forward and moved her hands slightly. She looked down on them and what they held…then changed the relative positions of the two objects and held the bottle over the glass….

"Yes, come along!" her husband said. "Are you going to be all day giving it me?"

With a jerk, she poured the liquid out into a glass and handed it to him. She looked away—towards the door….

"Ah, your way of escape!" said he, following her eyes. Then he drank, painstakingly.

The empty bottle fell out of her hands. She wrung them, murmuring—

"Oh, if I had only known!"

"Known what? That I should go near to cursing you for bringing me back?"

He fixed his cold eyes on her, as the liquid passed slowly over his tongue….

"—Or that you would end by taking back the gift you gave?"

Made in the USA
Middletown, DE
19 January 2021